The past has gone.

Time is the keeper.

Also by Neil Stanners -

'The Magic Room'

'Visions'

'Somewhere Night Falls'

Assigned Climes

NEIL STANNERS

Published by Garamonde 2019

GARAMONDE

International distribution.
Copyright (Text and Covers) Neil Stanners 2019
The moral right of the author has been asserted.

ISBN 978-1-86275-002-9

Production by Media Services
Cover photo: Helen Tu

Neil Stanners was born in Sydney.

He lived and worked in Europe.

He now resides once again in Sydney.

CONTENTS

Preface

Short stories are often long stories that have not yet matured.
They live in an abridged version of their possibilities.
So it is with this collection. Most started as the germ of an idea with promise. Then they ran their course so neatly that it would have been cruel to add words and deviations to the storyline in order to turn them into more complex versions of themselves.
They all live as small pieces of life, each with a simple window to a time and place where the characters play out their roles and a conclusion is reached and we bid them farewell.
When you leave be sure to say goodbye.

Neil Stanners

ASSIGNED CLIMES

There is a noise. Soft bells? And my stomach alerts me to a change of direction. Dropping, falling. My neck hurts and my mouth is open. I'm not yet ready to move.

.... "apologises once again for our late departure. You are assured that full ground facilities and ongoing transport will be available upon arrival."

Oh, dropping like a rock. Quick descent. Pilots anxious to be elsewhere.

"Please place your seat in the upright position, sir. Here let me help."

She's leaning across to me.

"You snored."

Who said that?

The old gentleman through my blinking eyes is glaring.

He has positioned himself carefully. In the next seat, yet above and away, as if viewing a bad accident.

"Sleep. It's one of my little vices I'm afraid. The snoring, I'm not sure I do but it could be the injury I suffered in combat."

A lie of course. It was a broken nose playing football.

Cabin crew have retreated quickly to their bulkhead seats. A squeak, a bump, with emphatic timing we are down and taxiing rapidly. Buried in the seat pocket looking for nothing. Can I hold off my neighbour's open mouth and continued exasperation?

Saved. The flight attendant is back at her job after the landing, moving down the aisle. God they're in a hurry. Perhaps a party at the crew's hotel.

My bag arrives first off the plane. The camera bag comes last. The bus has gone and there are no taxis. Everybody wants to be gone.

Secured in the split leather seats of an old Mercedes, with a finely negotiated price, I am in the hands of free enterprise and travelling along a palm-lined road close to the ocean. It turns to a dirt road. Awaiting my arrival is the Star Nest Hotel or if this late-night, out of the shadows, "would you like a ride, sir" person, is not as he seems, perhaps a robbery in the ricefields.

His demeanour is engaging. An amiable character. Surely no thief and criminal could have such a range of topics or manner of delivery.

It's a stucco, once white, three-story building with an extensive balcony on each level. In the foyer a single globe glows through the grubby panes of the closed and locked front doors. Jimmy Luck in the office recommended it. After I had rung and booked, he confided that he had not seen his homeland in twenty years. The same twenty years since the war ended and our editorial committee decided it would make a nice feature piece to revisit the troops old staging areas.

The Mercedes has sped away leaving me and my cases on these dark front porch steps. A cane lounge off to the side might be a place to sleep until morning.

There is no buzzer to ring. A black, spider-trap hole where the button once protruded.

A tinkle on the cute brass, manual bell, hanging above, brings shuffling feet.

"Ah, ah, ah, Mr Cain," he says, unlatching the door, "now we can both go to bed." He's beaming that disconcerting Asian way that masks any valid interpretation of the situation.

"I snore."

"Of course."

Green and yellow. An eye, large and black, within my security range. It squawks.

"Jesus Christ!"

Upright, heart pounding. A huge parrot has lifted the mosquito net and is examining me from the bedside table.

"You leave bal ………."

"Jesus Christ!"

The man from last night is on the other side of the bed. He has a tray.

"Parrot curious. You leave balcony doors open." He shoo shoos the bird away. It moves somewhat truculently and takes to flight in a casual manner.

The breakfast has two soft poached eggs, saffron rice and a mix of greenery in a light brown sauce. There's also a steaming cup of green tea.

Sans parrot, the doors shut, the proprietor departed, sitting, sipping my tea I am coming to terms with the Star Nest Hotel.

As a counterbalance to my late arrival I have slept well into the morning. It is an aspect of the travelling life I find secretly quite enjoyable. A type of Xmas-morning feeling of waking in a strange place and discovering the surroundings and the good or bad that it offers. There have been some bads, some very bads. The Star Nest seems to be a good but let's not be hasty.

"Well, 'bout time you come down. S'pose you want bed
made. Where is breakfast tray?"

My friend. The only man I have seen at the Star is behind
his counter, reading a newspaper, smoke curling round his
face from an odd, lumpy cigarette. He is skinny and bald
and wearing all black and sandals. He could be anywhere
between thirty and sixty. Another Asian thing.

The foyer is deserted and dim. Cane chairs spread about on
a huge square of possibly once Afghan carpet. A fan with
one of its four blades absent circles slowly overhead. Brown
wood walls, dusty, the sun cutting a gold rectangle in the
doorway. There are numerous possible replies.

"You must work very hard for the uncaring, selfish guests."

His face brightens, down goes the cigarette.

"It is so hard," he says, "they want everything ...."

"I came down to ask where you like the breakfast trays to be
left."

He shows me down a corridor to a hatch and small kitchen.
An incredibly old woman is removing the feet of several
ducks. Arthritic hands. Thwack. Remember to check for
fingers in my lunch.

Back in the foyer.

"I'm going for a walk. To look around. Look at the town."

He sighs."Okay, we'll go and 'look' at the town." Gives a
phlegm-filled cough and snorting laugh. "There is no fucking
town. Americans blew it up. This place was their brothel so

they left it. This and some others."

Don't know how my statement of intent became an invitation but by hell, he's right. The Star nest is alone. Outside, standing with this short man and his cigarette, we have rubble, fields, tree-lined streets and many makeshift dwellings. Piles of French colonial bricks everywhere with foliage reclaiming the lost land.

"Why?"

"I don't know. Probably had some leftover explosives. This place was full of corrupt people. Money-crazed, slimes. Sell their grandmother. Just like real Americans. Must have been drunk or had the wrong map."

"How many guests do you have at your hotel?"

"You make number four. I'm overcharging you to get a little extra. Your stinking company can afford it."

He was right.

As we walk. "So why you here anyway, Mister?"

"You can call me James."

"You can call me 'Sir'." He nearly chokes on his joke and spits violently in the dust.

"Official reason I'm here. Photos and some notes of the area where Australians were based. Spread in the March issue. Secretly I want to check something my father told me."

"Of course, fucking Australians. Bigger pain in the arse than Americans. No money."

Round a battered, bullet-holed white wall. Green vines, palms and wreckage. A store with lots of produce out the front. The weird fruit that Asians love. Coca Cola, tins of corn, bamboo shoots, bottles of sauces, pots, pans, utensils. He slaps the wall. "This was rich doctor. He got out. Fix lots of soldiers with 'diseases'. He now in America."
So I took some angled shots with the wall on one side. Good for a background to a feature header. Down the street, two storey colonial buildings with verandahs. Obviously deserted.

"Are those the whorehouses?"

"Girls used to hang over balconies with their titties out."
The main street has hints of a delightful French colonial past. Now seriously neglected. Another shop. Dim inside. Crammed with cheap junk. More pots, pans and plastic items. Freezer with ducks and pigs in vacuum-sealed packs. Few more establishment shots.

"So the Star Nest got involved. You know, in the trade."

"For a while. Making big money. But fucking soldiers keep trashing the place. One night I get the shits. Get gun. Tell them all to piss off. Big mistake. I could be in America now."

He turns in front of me. Scrawny, bloodshot eyes, those rotten teeth, grinning.

"So what your father tell you? Some good secret? He leave some gold bars somewhere?"
I don't want to answer. Why should I? Don't like or trust him.

A group of those parrots screech overhead. I'm looking, he's grinning in my face. Wish I hadn't told him.

"Which was Le Palais de Rose?"

"Aahhh?"

"I need to see inside."

The place still has doors. Huge carved things with four hinges. Too big to steal. Everything else is gone.

"So what we looking for?"

"Hey, that's my business."

"Hey, I your friend."

"No you're not. You're the owner of a cheap, nasty old hotel and former whorehouse in a forgotten Vietnamese village. And you're hanging around because you can smell money or some situation to your advantage."

He looks at me with that same Asian grin. He shrugs.

"Yeah, you right."

Impossible to insult these guys. I think I like him a little.

We found the first one on the wall on the first floor. It would have been behind the absent door. Scratched into the plaster with a knife. My doubts are dispelled. My father really was here.

He scowls. "Duyen? Girl name, mean graceful or something."

In the toilet, where the sink has been ripped from the wall, is the word 'Pham.' Shakily etched in the plaster. Same hand.

I'm taking a few interior shots as we go. Need to create a

story that will keep head office happy.

"Just name," he says. "Why your father scratch name Pham Duyen on walls? He mad or something? Malaria maybe. Or real crazy, start to like whore too much. Big mistake."

It takes some minutes to find the third on my father's list. Dust and dirt on the concrete floor have filled it in. But it's where he said it would be.

"Cho Son. It up the coast. Nice place. Small. Farmers. What all this about? He love this girl or something? Like I say that never go well. Soldier and local whore."

"I've got one more to find."

On the back of the building. Two big palms. Still there. On the base of one in the trunk. 'Teahouse.'

Walking back, the proprietor of the Star Nest is suddenly animated. Uses my name in a circuitous move on the truth.

"So James. He leave treasure at teahouse with this girl? You think that it? My help has been invaluable."

"Oh yeah. You're a saint. He wrote the messages in case he was wounded. So he'd have something to go on if he ever came back. Lot of the lads took 'stuff' to help with the anxiety and that could cause memory loss."

"Oh that smart. What if he forget he even wrote the messages?"

"Well he didn't. He had a card with info that would locate

the places he'd written his clues. Would mean nothing to anybody who found it. As it was he remembered writing something on the walls. Just couldn't remember what they said or why he wrote them. He suffered a head wound. Was shipped out. Bits of the time here keep coming back to him. Now he wants me to find out what he wrote and what they mean. I think he hopes there's some loot."

"Ah loot. That good James."

Lunch was very much like breakfast. With some fried duck added, though I did get the coffee I requested. I ate in my room to avoid 'Sir'. I could tell the bastard was watching me.

"When we go to Cho Son? Not far. Soon eh?"

"I may not go. Seems those messages don't mean much. I've got a photo assignment to get done. Going to have an after-lunch sleep."

I gave it half an hour. Checked the silence.

From the balcony it was quite easy to hop down to the lower level and then to the ground. From the back of the Star Nest a track took me to the road and from there into the town.

I bought a coke at the first shop and asked the woman where I could hire a motorbike.

"No motro bike. Just car."

"A car would be fine. Where do I go?"

"Here," she says, going round the corner of her establishment, sweeping some chickens away and pulling a dusty canvas from a lump outside in a corner which becomes a little white Citroen. Possibly the first one ever sold in Vietnam. Her husband pumps the tyres scowling. Driving out from the car's tin shed I nearly run over the proprietor of the Star Nest.

"Come to meet you. Save picking me up."

On the coastal road. Pretty farms.

"Seeing I have you with me again. What is your name?"

"Okay too hard for you to say. Also embarrassing in Vietnamese so just call me 'bloke' or something."

"Did your parents hate you? Look I'll call you 'sir'. It can be our little joke."

He grins. Seems to like the situation.

"Okay James. You good guy."

Cho Son is bigger than expected. It's all farming. Men moving about with produce, chatting, talking, women with children, tractors pulling trailers of produce, the usual hundreds of motorbikes, activity everywhere. One bustling, noisy main street. Everybody driving with the use of the horn and accelerator.

"There's a teahouse. That must be it."

"It could be. If you very lucky. There another teahouse. There two more. Pretty sure that one as well."

"They drink a lot of tea in these parts?"

"Tea for day, alcohol for night."

Blank looks at the first teahouse.

"Pham Duyen? No, nobody here. You want tea."

The girl smiles as if she knows more. Or is it just me? The tea is nice. I even buy 'sir' some banh bao.

"We can't drink tea in every one of these."

Sir strokes his chin. "We just ask. No harm to ask. Lot of years though. Girl your father know dead, lost, moved, married ..... who knows."

No luck at the second. More blank looks at the third. Round the corner a neat little shop selling food. A few tables and chairs outside.

"Is this a teahouse?"

"No harm to ask, James. Maybe a little rivalry. Teahouse people not tell about other teahouse, so this not teahouse so no rivalry."

The woman is suspicious. "Why you have questions? Who you? You want food?"

I take a look at the smiling countenance of 'sir'.

"She didn't say no."

"You right, James," he says and breaks into Vietnamese.

He doesn't charm her. I suspect he's too old and ugly but after a lengthy chat the woman goes to the back of the shop and retrieves a pencil and paper.

Outside once more.

"What?"

"She bought the shop from Duyen about ten years ago. When she did the woman live at this address. Just up road here. We drive."

It takes longer. Streets are not all marked and much asking and wrong information or too helpful information leads us astray. Plus I'm obliged to take some more magazine shots. 'Sir' is disgusted that I take shots that are not of the place in the assignment.

"So you believe everything you read in the press?"

"Well no, they all lying bastards."

Eventually with the right street confirmed several times we are able to make our way to the house that is pointed out. Those that give us this final direction have grave looks on their faces. It is a neat street with white stone walls and gates on most of the dwellings. The number on the wall is correct.

"Now for treasure."

I look at 'sir'.

"Been good to have you along. Don't get your hopes up. My Dad just wasn't a soldier of fortune. I think we'll meet a lady who might fondly remember him. If we're lucky we might be offered some tea or even a beer. Then we'll reminisce and be on our way."

"Or your Dad surprise you."

The wall is about shoulder height. Through the black painted gates the place is tidy with a vegetable patch, some ducks, even a pond full of large gold carp. Halfway to the door of the house along a pebble path 'sir' touches my arm. He indicates with his head to a small altar with incense burning and food on offer.
"Somebody may have died, James."
It is then that we see two young people standing on the path in front of us. They are male and female, quite handsome and probably in their early twenties. They are smiling quite broadly and looking at me like excited children.

On the trip back to the Star Nest 'sir' keeps bursting into fits of giggles.
Glaring at him makes no difference.
"He just have to know," the man says in between further bursts of laughter. "What your mother think? When you tell him. Can I listen? I get out some good US whiskey. Help build up your courage."

After tea, which is surprisingly good and several large tumblers of US whiskey I retreat to my room with a blanket ban on any eavesdropping.
The phone line is clear despite the feeling that 'sir' is listening in, somewhere down below.

My father answers quite quickly. I've decided on a direct
approach with the information. No foreplay.

"Dad, I followed up your messages. Amazing. Found them
all where you'd scratched them. Must admit I was sceptical.
Easier than I'd anticipated. It was quite weird thinking you
were here when I was young. I now know what they mean.
Went to a town called Cho Son. Do you remember Cho Son?
Duyen came from Cho Son? She worked in the kitchen at Le
Palais de Rose. They were planning to use her as a whore.
You gave her the money to buy a teahouse, to get out.
I found that teahouse. It's now a cafe. I went to her home.
We didn't meet her, Duyen died about two months ago."

I allowed a slight pause for that part of my message to be
absorbed.

From the earpiece I heard only, "Oh."

"Dad, it seems that 22 years ago Duyen gave birth to twins.
A girl and a boy. They were part Caucasian. I met them. Our
meeting was both a joyous and a sad occasion. Duyen waited
all her life for word from you.

I came too late. But now, with her passing the twins are
relieved of further responsibilities in caring for their mother.
And they are very excited. You have made contact at last.
They're very anxious to travel to meet their father and
live with him. Seems you made that firm and unshakeable
promise to Duyen when you last saw her and she told you
she was with child.

So Dad, when I return next week I'll be bringing Minh and

Tuan home to be with you. How do you feel about that Dad? Make a hell of a good feature story."

There was silence on the other end of the phone.

"Dad, you there? Dad?"

SEAVIEW

$\mathbf{A}$t the big house that father and mother had bought, that mother had left, that father had then remodelled for his chair, where time was a captive, Ben sat, as Camilla prepared lunch and sang in that soft jolly tone she adopted when concerned by the silence and creaking of the boards in the summer heat.

"Open the windows, Benjamin."

"Then I would hear the waves and smell the ocean. I don't want that."

Father had lost heart. This room, the big one in front, facing the ocean, is not furnished.

"There seems no point, Ben. You understand. More space for your wheels, anyway."

"I'm doin' chicken, Benny. You okay with that?"
"Sounds fine Camilla." Her voice starts again then stops.
"You by the window?"
"Yeh."
"You're gonna melt."

Nothing for a moment. Ben counts eight seconds holding his fingers up. He drops his hand in a starting motion and Camilla begins to sing again, way off in the kitchen.

Yes, he is by the window. They are bay windows. There was a blanket box seat under the window. Father had it removed to allow the chair to get right up close. On the wall, his tyre marks make black stripes down the white lime wash woodwork.
"No point cleaning them off anymore, you're just gonna put more back. Wonder if you can get white rubber?"

From the garden, there are two rows of almost perfect she-oaks forming a surreal walking path away down the slope. They end at the sand. Leftovers from the old house that was removed to make way for their mansion. The line is long. They appear to merge like a desert railway.

Father has gone. He is at home as little as possible. A small city apartment instead. "There is no point", he says, avoiding the eyes of his son. Camilla is the answer. A woman from the town who is able to live in while her husband is at sea. Sometimes father's absence and her husband's return create a dilemma.

"Can't leave you here Ben. No, don't start with any of your tough-guy stuff. How would I feel if anythin' was to happen to you?"
Ben is bundled into the old Volvo and taken down to the town and Camilla's little cottage.
"What's that bloody kid doin' here? For Christ's sake honey, you can't be wet nursin' every stray in town. I've been away for nearly eight weeks. We need a bit of bloody privacy. It's not like I can send him outside to play, I mean is it? What's the matter with his old man anyway?"
Whispering.
"Yeh, I'll be nice to him. Okay, Jesus!"

This day is still. Those soft tree branches lift a little in occasional movements of air. Ben imagines the earth turning as it lays in the sun and a small breath escaping its lips.
He is looking down the line of trees. Very intently, making out the furthest reaches of the path. His knuckles on the chair are white. Like the day, he appears to have no breath. His eyes have lost their focus.

Hard and sweating, biting his lip. A slight tremor through his body. The brush of an oak frond on his cheek. Floating between these whispering, wallowing branches. High up, or is it just the unusual notion of being upright.

He grasps the trees and pieces break away. Fragile tips that sprinkle the ground.

As the end comes closer there is an involuntary speeding up. The last comes with a rush. It is In sight, that glare, the noise, the roar. Oh, that sound that only waves can make.

Starting, looking about. Jerked back, he is in the chair. Outside is the world. Inside is the sound of Camilla coming along the hallway with her singing and chicken sandwich.

"Christ Benny, you been having one of your turns?" She looks down at his sweating pale face. She calls them 'turns'. He has no need to explain. Escaping, that's what he would say. If I think hard enough I can escape.

"I don't give a shit what the doctors say. Sumpthin' ain't right." Hand on the brow. "Hmmm."
A short exhalation.
"C'mon let's get you out of the sun. You can eat in the dining room. Ben. Ben. How many fingers am I holding up?"
"Twelve."
"You're okay, I guess."

Ben could go outside. There were runways, beautifully structured and smooth, on all sides. Father has seen to that. Ramps and paths run across the grass, round ponds, near flowers and under trees. Planned and executed with great care. Always in close proximity to the indoors.

Beyond the paths is the soft, beckoning roll of green covered, headland soil. Waiting, off the edge of the boy's existence, always there. Its presence is stressfully obvious. Fingers can reach down and touch it. Hands can be run over it. It exudes a calming, waiting, wanting knowledge of the predicament. A knowledge that its texture can entrap and hold whatever weight is placed upon it. Just off the path, just off the path.

The house is a desert island, surrounded by a deceptive sea.

On father's visits, in the awkward silence of the big lounge, the words do not come out.

"Is the tutor happy with your work?"

"Yes, I guess he is."

"Good. He was highly recommended you know. Previous satisfied customers. Got their grades up, sorted out learning issues, you know the sort of thing."

They are there in his stomach, they rise in his throat, float on his tongue. Those words. Some are ready to slip past his teeth as he inhales. It is the leap into sound that they cannot make.

"Father, am I a prisoner here? Or is it just that it hasn't

occurred to you?"
In the still air, they fall empty on his father's chair. The man
is already driving hurriedly away. Back to the city, where he
can work and pretend. The damned accident. The look of
disappointment on his father's face. So much happened that
night in his father's eyes as he sat by the bed. Mother would
not come to the hospital. She knew already that this changed
the balance. Their perfect child was no longer perfect.
Ben considered later the implications of having a child. Had
it been a family pet, a dog perhaps, the matter would have
been so much simpler. Clean the slate. Go buy another. But
father had to talk her into a 'child'.

Camilla fussed. She hovered.
"It's not like I'm paid for this. There's no dollars in this for
me."
She resented the situation and grew angry with herself
at the involvement she drew from this simply advertised
housekeeping job.
"Damn the man. Damn him." The words are muttered, out of
hearing, with no malice.

She takes him shopping. Wrestled him into the car and with
the chair hanging from the boot they drive away from the
local town to some other anonymous, larger place.
"Shopping's better here," she says.
Flour, milk, margarine. Staples available at the corner

grocery. It is guilt.

"You're a fool to take that boy on, Camilla. Why get involved? Just do your job. Nobody is going to thank you."

So they shopped in a distant place.

He laughed sometimes on these outings. At silly things. Often his jokes were beyond her understanding but she smiled along dumbly happy to see him, momentarily free. He was a smart kid. Though never obvious about his intellect. On the trips he grew silent and quite sullen if interrupted, along the ocean road. Once she took a different route to see if there would be a reaction. He said nothing for a while staring straight ahead after she turned away from the coast.

Near the end of one trip as she concentrated on parking, he said, "God you must hate this."

Glancing back over her shoulder she saw a look of such despair that she lay for some weeks after, staring at night into that same face, hearing the tenure of his voice.

A picnic in the National Park produced mixed results. The day had a blustery, cool breeze that kept others away. They invited the tutor, who, to their surprise accepted. There was the impression that he had never sat on the ground before. Afterwards he threw a ball to Ben but was so inaccurate that the farce became distressing as the boy reached vainly for the thing as it sailed past. Once home, a rare moment.

"He is the most boring man I have ever met," Camilla

ventured.

It was a reckless comment. She had no feel for the relationship between student and teacher. Ben looked at her and closed his eyes.

"Please, please, never invite him on anything again."

In this secret moment, they both laughed. The woman's hands lifted to embrace. She wiped them on her apron instead and went to the kitchen.

Each day of this new month brought a movement in the barometer. Ben studied the rises in pressure in the glass, of the thing on the wall. Not for any great meteorological interest, simply that it was there. Like the weather forecasts on TV or online.

The connections were where the project stopped. So many things in this house were there, waiting for a completion that now would not come. Ben had changed everything.

The heat crept into the wood and stayed. Unable to be shaken out now until the cooler months of autumn.

Camilla helped with his showers. Father talked of air conditioning but it had not been installed. With his interest in the being close to the window and in the sun, she insisted on 'cleanliness' of at least a two-day cycle.

A compromise had established itself without negotiation.

A plastic chair was in place in a shower. He allowed himself to be undressed but retained his shorts. Once in the shower with the screen closed he wrestled the remaining garment over his useless legs and off. This act had the dual action of retaining some dignity in his small life and reminding him of how utterly hopeless he had become. There was no escape. Here was the evidence.

Alone at these times with the water cascading over his face and body he often granted himself a tiny indulgence. Head bowed, looking down at the remains of his manhood, he cried. For some time he let this act clean his grief, safely hidden in the water. He fingered his knees, touched his skin, examined his body and its situation and sobbed at the hopelessness of it all. He bit his thumbs and his arm to keep the act silent, as silent as possible.

Did the woman know?

She checked of course. "You washing in there or gone to sleep?"

Eventually, he did wash. It took ages to dry himself. She threw a towel over the screen. Then powder and dry shorts. Finally, out she dried his legs and finished by wiping his face and back.

"You got soap in your eyes again. You've got to rinse properly, fella." An encouraging smile as she tried to have him look at her. He worried her. If you could hold up your hand and block the bottom half of the image then he was still there. This perfect boy. Handsome beyond belief. Dark hair, dark eyes and what could be a heart-stopping smile.

He longed, of course, to tell her of his wish to go to the beach. He did not because he knew she would take him. To the beach, not the water. And that would be worse. A giant sweet shop with no money. Perhaps she knew. She observed. Perhaps she was afraid. It was not her job. Simply a housekeeper. Her husband might have forbidden it. "For Christ's sake girl. Get some sense into you. What if anything happened? Just do the job you're paid for and leave it at that."

Ben had a room. It was to have been the master bedroom. Father changed the configuration afterwards. His attempts at patching the mess compounding in the boy's mind, his guilt. So this large room with views across the lawn became a boy's dream. Materially he had much to like. Sound, vision, stimulation of the mind were all given quite major input. Alone with all these toys the boy idled and did nothing. He lay for hours on his bed at times, listening to grand stirring symphonies. Dvorak's 'New World' brought a lump to his throat. Londonderry Aire had the sort of melancholy in which he could hide. Father had made final payments on the house eight weeks before the accident. Work on the fit-out was underway when it happened. The compromise for moving away from his friends had always been that they could visit and stay as often as they liked. None had ever been. He thought he did not want it and father had forgotten the pledge.

What if they came? What could they do? Sit and talk. He looked normal. No scars or disfigurement. The legs that once carried him as they joked their way around the neighbourhood, stepped and dodged in ball games, ran, climbed, fell, scarred, were now simply growths on the end of his body. The embarrassed silences, saying the wrong things, sympathy. He lived it all. Imagining every detail of their arrival, stay and departure.

At one side of the house with a great sweep of tiles leading up to it, is the garage. Enough room for three cars. The big doors are electrically operated. He enters through the side access door. Sunlight from the early morning spreads his shadow across the big empty space. His head is pointed. The wheels seem huge. A mockery of his condition.

At the left-hand end, a big area partitioned off. There is a bench in place and many tools fixed in position. It is as if everybody has been called away to tea. Boxes half-open. Crates and materials strewn about, waiting to be sorted. Those without a destination stacked against the wall. Much of the occupants of this section are the accoutrements of a planned male domain.

Ben begins his search at the bench. He quickly finds some tie wire and places it at eye level on the bench.

He pauses in his work and listens. She must not find him here. There will be questions and answers he does not wish

to give. She will cancel the project, not by force but with
stealth and reason and sense. He will be talked round. Now
he adds a tube of glue to the bench and some tape.
Moving further out through this sea of cardboard he reads
his way down the boxes stacked against the wall. They
are labelled. A service of the moving company. 'Books -
Cookery', 'Loungeroom lamp,' 'Wine Glasses,' 'Albums' ......
For a while, he stares at this last box. It is easy to reach,
stacked at the right height. Finally, he wheels over and pulls
it down onto its side. Moving the chair, he is able to nudge it
over. Picking with his fingernails he can tear off the packing
tape. He stops again looking at the box flaps. Why is he doing
this?
With a breath of resignation and the question unanswered,
he opens the box. Inside, standing with their spines upright
are a series of smartly bound books, each with their
contents and year neatly written. They are in chronological
order. Somebody has taken a lot of care.
The first book is dated before his birth, the rest come after.
Ben reaches down and pulls the centre book onto his lap.
It is here that he stops again. With his elbows on the plush
cover and his head in his hands, his eyes search the far wall
as he ponders the situation before him. For some minutes he
is unmoving.
With a grunt of finality, he snaps back to the present,
grabs the pages with his left hand and opens the album
to its centre. There he is. A large colour print. Standing

on the edge of a beach with the white water of a wave
breaking around his legs. He is wet and grinning happily at
the camera, his hands outstretched. Strangely he cannot
remember the photo being taken, yet there is this person,
who has a rapport with the photographer. They are sharing
the moment.

Like his friends, he has all the gear that goes with the beach.
Unlike his friends he often simply swam and bodysurfed. It
was being there that mattered. Feeling the water, being in the
waves.

He turns to other pages. There are many family photos.
He features in most. Hikes, picnics, a birthday party. He feels
like an intruder. They are the history of another person. Who
is this kid and why can he not remember most of what he
sees?

He replaces the album and takes another. The one from the
right- hand side of the box. The one with the most recent
date. Once again he does not want to look. Pausing before
curiosity compels him. He opens it to the middle. The pages
are blank. He works his way back. Somewhere near the front
of the book photos appear. They are of the trip they had
made to the mountains. Their last together. When mother
had decided to head back early, to take care of some final
packing, while the boys did something adventurous.

She must have ordered the prints and put them into the
album immediately because it had only been three days later
that it happened.

Ben has been at his task for over an hour. He is keen to finish. Camilla is due to do one of her periodic sweeps of the area to check that he is okay. There at the bottom a box, he locates the main item of his search. He rolls over to the bench and places a coil of flat rubber belting next to the wire, glue, tape and a pair of pliers. Time to get out. During this operation he has misjudged his strength or the weight of some of the high boxes, twice toppling over and out of his chair. The tedious task of dragging himself and the chair, with gritted teeth to the bench, in order to regain his seat, has left the boy dirty and tired.

Finally outside with the garage door just closed Camilla approaches with a drink in her hand.

"I thought you might be thirsty."

"Thanks, I am."

It is a game. An excuse to find him. He takes the glass and drinks. She cares and that counts a lot. Occasionally she forgets herself and touches his cheek. Life is a mixture of posturing. All playing parts and hiding the truth. If she could say and he could say. And father and mother. But then the situation is his fault.

Sometimes he wants to ask her to just hold him for a while. But he can't. Contact remains a fluttering unsatisfying moment when both long for more.

He must study. That is the excuse. It is plausible. He is

neglecting his lessons. Camilla needs some 'things' in town.
At the window he watches her car swing out of the gates.
He'll wait. There is a period where she may turn back for
something she has forgotten. Past that point, she will not be
bothered.

After a suitable time, he rolls his way down the ramp, out of
the house and round to the garage door. Pressing the remote
it rumbles up.

The sky is deep blue. Drawn across the end of the horizon
a dark mass of clouds has come from inland. It gives the
landscape a strange contrasting light so admired by last
century's European painters.

In the town, Camilla is talking to an earnest man in the Pet
Shop. To a background of fish tanks and curious guppies,
they are discussing dog breeds and which will be best suited
to the 'situation'. With a decision made the pup is put into
a cardboard box for the trip, along with a new collar. Why
is she doing this? It will be more work and she can't really
afford it. Perhaps the father will recompense her in gratitude.

In the garage, Ben is laying on the floor next to his chair.
He has cut strips of hard, flat rubber to fit past the
circumference of the wheels. Wrapped his wheels then taped
and glued the strips in place finally using wire through the
spokes. With these strips on the wheels, the load will be
spread. Softer soil will be accommodated.

Last week the Tutor had looked at him in the middle of
a lesson. He fought to maintain the boy's interest as he
explained the simple physics. Ben had heard it all. His blank
expression hid the thought processes involved in examining
the potential of the application.

Overnight a storm has moved through and off the coast.
In its passing, in the night, it has worked with the high tide
to venture far up the beach. With a flick of its tail, it has
created a wall. Halfway to the water, the sand is banked quite
dramatically right along the beachfront. The wall and all the
sand in this early morning, is damp and hard. Spray hisses
off the breakers as they pound in, disturbed by the activity
of the night, restlessly surging up and dropping away. With
the promise of bright sun, it is the start of a joyous day.
Already the heat is in the air.
Poised at the top of the sand ridge, breathing the air, the feel
and the view Ben is poised, his wheels hanging over. He has
a clear run to the water.

It is Camilla who, on one of her hunch checks, begins to
circle the rooms of the house. The pup is still in the car.
She wants them to meet. Exhausting the possibilities and
receiving no answer to her calls she moves outside. He has
been messing about in the garage lately. Yes. Inside there is
evidence of activity. Pieces of wire and rubber. Tools and a

knife laying about.

"Ben! Where are you? Answer me." He can't be far. She is slightly nervous. He is not the type to play games with people.

Walking round the big place following the paths, calling. Now, her self- imposed burden, the responsibility, raises a slight panic. Where can he go, for Christ's sake?

For a while, she stands looking at the two lines that are clearly defined in the soil, between the rows of she-oaks. They lead to the beach. It is not possible for his chair to traverse this soft soil. While the truth of this matter has never been discussed it is a factor in her composure when minding Ben.

Standing, looking, the garage, the tools, the trail leading off, take time to present their case. Then she is running, struggling in the sand, her hand to her mouth.

Right there, through the end of the trees, across the grassy rise, the two marks continue. Down onto a ridge of sand on the beach. Her eyes race ahead. They follow the line which runs straight to the water.

His chair is over. Water pushing it about. From this distance, all of the situation is immediately clear. Her heart pounding, looking up and down the empty landscape, Camilla drops to her knees on the ridge. A noise, a sigh, a groan escapes

her lips like a hard punch. What she wishes to know is the motive. What a nice kid. Was he trapped by his enthusiasm? Did he venture too far? The alternative? He has escaped!
He has solved everyone's problems.

Rising, she now runs because she must, making her way down the steep sand.
Across the beach, in the water, at the end of the two lines in the sand, there is shape under the waves, lifting and falling in the morning tide.

THE APPLICANT

Subdued lighting sliced intermittently by blocks of daylight
from high above to the right. A rather nervous entry. Huge
doors that give a whoosh of pneumatic efficiency as they
open. Very plush carpet down a path to reception. Spongy
unsteady tread. The remaining floor is cream marble.
A tapestry on the high, marble wall. A predominance of deep
blue and purple. The atmosphere is library-hushed despite
the massive atrium.

The receptionist is just a dot on approach. A little head
engulfed by a high, impressive piece of reception furniture.
She appears uneasy. She whispers.

Leaning forward.

"Pardon?"

"Mr. Flain would like you to wait for a minute. Um, something came up."

"Pardon, what came up?"

"Something."

"Oh."

The applicant backs away. He wants to smile but it does not seem right. The receptionist is unreceptive. A fragile bird captured by her reception fortress.

There is a long, black leather lounge at a distance near the outer glass walls. It squeaks and hisses when weight is applied. There are magazines just out of reach. Concentrate on the moment.

The top of the receptionist's head moves about. Is she busy? There are not many calls.

Minutes pass by.

She stands briefly and glances up catching his eye. Is she smiling? He can't tell. He can't hear her speak on the phone. No wait, there is a faint sound, like neighbours in some nearby apartment.

Fifteen more minutes pass. He counts each one carefully.

Then she is standing, beckoning. At the desk, leaning over, she looks serious.

"There's still a problem. Mr. Flain is annoyed." She whispers.

"With me?" He also speaks very softly.

"No, - about his problem."

"Oh, - it's a big one then."

"Pardon?"

"The problem."

"Yes."

She's distracted.

"Right - I'll wait. Over there." He points. She nods.

She seems really flustered. Odd, it's a very big company. Seamless efficiency surely.

This time he takes a magazine as he sits.

'Frozen Foods Monthly.' It is quite thin and contains a lot of press release material. In the centre there is a colour spread with some brands he recognises.

Rolled to a tube he taps the magazine aimlessly until the girl stands, looking about. Whoops. Her eyes tell him nothing.

Ten minutes, no, eleven.

A faint vibration. The main doors slide back. A woman, striding so fast the doors have had just enough time to get out of her way.

Mid-thirties, tight striped suit, briefcase.

At reception they talk. He is the subject. The woman looks in his direction, then peels away and carries on through another door and away down a corridor. He can't see where she has gone.

Something must happen on this level even though the elevators indicate that all the important stuff is skyward.

Dammit. He rises, struggling out of his seat and leans forward over the magazine table, determined to find something of interest. The receptionist is watching.

Their eyes meet. Is that a frown? Just a magazine after all. She must have to stand periodically for reassurance or orientation. He sits. The lounge hisses and whines.

The lounge is too low. He feels vulnerable, unable to rise quickly if the need arose.

He still has 'Frozen Foods Monthly' - now also 'Container Freight News.'

Let's see. Big ships coming. Big ships going. An article 'Loss of Containers at Sea'. No mention of the owners of the contents, their plight or recovery. The article is on the side of the shipping company and their inconvenience.

At the back a compilation of trivia. There is a wedding on a deck, a blonde, the first female pilot in Alaska and a survey of port facilities. None of the local ports rate very highly.

A pair of legs, just above the top of the magazine. Solid legs in stout, flat-soled shoes.

"Some coffee sir?"

She's smiling, has a trolley with biscuits. Round face, flushed cheeks.

"I'm waiting to see Mr. Flain, I'm not sure there's time."

"Milk and sugar, sir?" Was there a tiny, intake of breath? Some complicity there?

"Oh, well, just milk, yes, thank you. Nice and strong."

How did she manage to perambulate to his position in such complete silence? Now she has vanished back down that long corridor and the door has efficiently hidden her away once more.

Sipping the coffee, looking about. Impressive biscuits. Not the ordinary supermarket fare. Her eyes at reception pass over him. Quite beautiful. Aware for the first time of their brown depth. Even at this distance.

He ponders the importance of the whole face in an assessment of the owner's state of mind.

If he goes to the desk again he will take note. Does the body containing those eyes fulfill their promise?

Little noises float in and out of his immediate area. Like the faint voices of a very distant radio signal from a foreign land, momentarily in your room as you search the dial. Possibly the building plays games with its acoustics, to snatch small pieces of somebody's conversation on some level and patch it in to another part of its innards. He cannot make out the words only the tricky flexing in and out of their appearance.

Time check. Over half an hour gone. No, forty minutes.

This is a situation of balance. What inefficiencies create a company with such dreadful management of their time?

Is the lack of interest in his presence indicative of some deeper layer. A change of heart, no longer required. Let the man work it out.

Climbing again from the leather-hissing, insecurity seat. Upright and still holding the cup and these magazines to place on the table.

Would it be impertinent to pace? Imprudent to inquire? Improper to look outside, at the view, hands clasped? Arms folded. Displaying negativity. Back in the black leather clutches.

Thought games. The mind is dulling in this sensory-deprived area. One person has come through those doors to cross into this marble world with all its trappings of corporate fat. What silent workers they must be. Are they asleep or is their industry one of an incredible cerebral power that creates no exterior rattle?

Flain is an important man. This interview is rare. Wait on.

A check of the portfolio. Everything is there. (It was, from the night he received the letter.) Reviewed and read many times. Now the day is at hand.

The sound of a plane. Faint and far away. The building does leak a little of the world. Full of executives no doubt. Early flights, orange juice and laptops all clicking away.

'Oh, what was that?' Did I speak or think? There is a fine disturbance in his bowel. Not now!

That coffee! Should have refused. Dilemma. What to do? Desperation.

"Excuse me." She jumps. Oh, yes, she is delightful.
How could I have failed to take note of this. No doubt
nervous, concentrating. Never know how much power the
receptionist has over the inner linings of the corporate
intestines.
"Mr. Flain, ... ahh?"
She gives a mixed look. Exasperation, apology, concern?
"Mr. Flain has not communicated with me."
There is the opportunity to use silence, to have her squirm
just a little. Wriggle awkwardly in guilt by association with
this procrastinator. But matters are more pressing.
"Is there a toilet handy?"
She seems relieved.
"Certainly, that's no problem." Standing and leaning forward.
Delightful perfume, Clean sparkling hair. A moment that
cannot be enjoyed.
"Down here, past the lifts, there's a door. It's not obvious.
Set back."
He's off.
"Wait, sir, you'll need the key."

Absurd. Sitting in this pristine, marble cubicle. Now, of
course, will be the time that Flain calls for him. Caffeine has
triggered a scouring of his gut. He is drained. Nerves and
coffee. Feels pale. A touch to the forehead. Damp, clammy.
Flain is going to see a corpse.
The washbasin too, is marble. There are voluminous white

towels and scented soap. It is very quiet. That is what
is missing. Normally in corporate monoliths, there is a
sprinkling of faint music of indeterminate quality or style.
Deep breath. This is the chance of a lifetime. Let's look at the
creamy white shirt, burgundy patterned tie, faint stripe in
the grey suit. Hair fine, colour coming back. Survival.
At the end of this day, I will be alive and no worse for the
encounter. Life's a lottery. All I've done is bought a ticket.

"There's your key, Allise." Familiarity from her name badge.
"Thank you."
"Still no um .... word?"
Another mixture of signals. Exasperation perhaps. Directed
at whom? Sit down, you boring man? Or, I am a conspirator
tall young stranger, please take me away? I am a wild
songbird in a cage.
"No, not yet."
She adds as he backs away to that lounge. "Mr. Flain doesn't
like inquiries."

Should have taken a drink of water in the toilet. No longer in
a peak of mental stability. Examine the fingernails. An excuse
to check if the hand is shaking.
She's watching again. Now, that was a smile. I'm sure that
was a smile. Only the eyes but there was a slight crinkling
round the eye sockets and the gaze did not sweep away as
before.

Assessment made. He'll get the position therefore, it is okay to be friendly towards him. What did Neville Oxley say at that boardroom lunch for the minions.

"Don't dip your pen in the company ink."

He probably would have added.

"and especially with a lowly rated receptionist."

Oxley was also known for saying, "I'm just a simple guy but I have a wicked sense of humour."

In the silence that followed that utterance, he felt a horrible camaraderie with the others as they jointly pondered.

'No you're not. You're an idiot with a vindictive nature. You should stay away from alcohol because it exacerbates your problem.'

After a time somebody in the group had said, "Quite" and summarised the situation.

Oxley sat on his sanctity, preening away, oblivious to the subtlety.

Well to hell with office maxims of behaviour he would be available if this receptionist wished to take things further. Oxley and his ilk would be left far behind in the old firm.

Now that little indulgent reverie took care of near twenty minutes. Outside the city has settled into another day. Deals, wheels and back watching. Rush hour is over. Except in this place where it appears to have never started.

Perhaps there is an advantage to this situation. Flain will be obliged. His problem has caused him to keep somebody

waiting beyond the accepted norms of business ethics.
'Business ethics', now where did that come from? A hasty
decision tinged with guilt.
"You have the position. Start tomorrow. The receptionist
will show you everything. Now if you don't mind, I have a
problem to be getting on with."

She is standing but not looking at me. Holding the fine phone
mouthpiece. Talking, using her hands. Can't hear what.
This place swallows sound. Allise, slim beauty, what is it?
A siren? Did I hear a siren? Outside! Through the doors that
are too slow. Wheeling a trolley, urgently, off to the lifts, with
Allise leading the way.
Now I'm a rubbernecking tourist. Can see nothing once the
doors close. Allise my beauty, my soulmate, my confidant
has gone away with them, up to the sky.
Minutes pass. At reception the phone is indicating incoming
calls, that are going unanswered. Oh, this is crazy. Now I'm
alone in this giant receptacle. Captive and torn by indecision.
"I'm surprised you did not tactfully leave, sir. Was it not
obvious that Miss Tight Suit No.7 had cut her hand rather
badly on the doco shredder? You could have rung for
another appointment instead of gazing upon our misfortune.
Frankly, I'm disappointed."

Fretting. What to do? Has the situation reached absurd? Was
the slight smile earlier on, really a smile of pity? Time is not

right in this place. It moves as if held in slowly setting aspic.

Bing. Out they come. Such a rush. Get out of the way. Several important-looking people behind Allise and the paramedics and their cargo. All look like they could be having an affair with her. Outside, load up. Sirens going and away. Executives back through the doors in an earnest, talking bunch. Which one is Flain? Did he notice me?

Alone, centre of the foyer. Allise is back at her desk. No, she is not. She approaches. Wonderful legs.
"About your appointment," she says. Her face is hard to read. "I'm most terribly sorry but it won't be possible now."
"Oh dear," I say, "is Mr. Flain upset over the accident? That's okay I can come tomorrow."
A pause. Pursed lips. Then in a non-committal voice.
"No, Mr. Flain was the accident. He is no more. There is no tomorrow. I am sorry."
Allise walks back and I would like to look but now there is a new priority. I am being consumed by a pure, burning slice of motivation. To be somewhere else. Outside and gone.

THE LAST TIME

Do you know Reynolds Park? The little grassy spot up the hill, at the end of Maxime Crescent? Don't be concerned, there are few who do know the place. With its rusty swings, bird-spotted picnic table, weeds, decay and that ominous big lump of sandstone laying there.
Some say they heard the huge rock rumble down from the cliff late at night all those years ago. Even so, it took days for the locals to notice its presence. Nobody wanted to go there after that event. Now Reynolds Park is mostly forgotten.

However, if you do know the park, you may also know the path and where it leads.

Maxime Crescent was new fifty years ago. The houses were all grand and neat and their owners were proud of their lovely street. A showpiece on the edge of town. The council established Reynolds Park on the perimeter of the bush reserve and then in a burst of further enthusiasm deduced that it would be feasible to create a lookout at the top of the cliffs above the street.

They put in a user-friendly path with all-weather stone steps all the way up from Reynolds Park. A large flat area was cleared back from the cliff edge and a host of European and North American trees were planted which gave the area a pleasant forested aspect. Finally, they designed a giant, pre-cast, family-sized, curved seat. Transported it up to the lookout in three pieces and bolted it all to a concrete slab. The path was then indicated by a small plaque in the park. For a while, many people made the steep climb to the lookout. Picnics took place and on occasions, ice-cream could be purchased before visitors began the ascent to the lookout. The view over the town and the trees and delightful big gully, full of birdsong, was worth the effort. There were few things more pleasant than watching the sunset or sunrise from the giant concrete seat.

Today the lookout is a forgotten experience. The path is almost lost except to those few who still know where to find its beginnings. The plaque has gone. Nature has moved back into the clearing claiming the grass, spreading leaves and broken branches. It is a tangled piece of bush again. The seat is still there once found. Overall the lookout is now a lonely world abandoned by the new people of the town.

At about 10am this clear, sunny day there is a sound at the top of the path. It is a surprise. A bird flutters up to the sky. Lizards dart from their warm rocks. Insects wait in frozen postures. The whole bushland pauses and waits. Following some more sounds of struggle, a man appears. He hesitates, looking about, gasping from the effort of the ascent.
He is not a young man. That is obvious. Leaning against a substantial white oak, his head lowered, he balances his breathing, dabbing his wet forehead with a blue handkerchief. He remains so for a while. Eventually, calmed and partly restored he raises his head. He looks about, taking in the familiar area.
He says something quietly. It sounds like, "I'm here, Alice."

The seat is still in place. The man can see the lump of grey, covered in all sorts of bush detritus. He makes his way in an irregular journey to its base, stepping over logs, skirting bushes, avoiding a boggy patch. With the flat of his hand, he sweeps away all the leaves and sticks, nuts and dried assorted bush oddments then seats himself comfortably in the middle. For a moment he takes a deep breath. A sound of satisfaction. Of achievement. Then he slowly scans the view, still delightful after so many years.

Wrestling himself back for maximum comfort he reaches into his small backpack and takes out some plastic-wrapped sandwiches, a bottle of water and finally a small towel that he places on the seat to his left with the food items on top. From the water bottle, he gulps half the contents before stopping and replacing the lid.

He looks about once more and draws in another large breath which he lets out slowly. It is hot and the climb was very taxing. Finally, he places his hands on his knees as if completing some preplanned ritual.

It is then that he begins to speak.

"You know Alice, I thought the other day ...." He stops, as if the import of his news is quite dramatic.

"I thought about the beginning and end of everything," he says slowly. He waits, letting his words hang in the air.

"It was a revelation. Unless in the universe there are some things with no end then it must be assumed that all things end. And of course, to end they must have had a beginning. It all must have a start. It can be no other way. For me, well, the first time I swam in the ocean, the first time I saw an elephant, first day of school, my first pay packet, the moment we met, our first-born, our last born...."

He paused.

"Such an idea. I started a list but after about ten pages of columns, I realised there were too many entries. Do you know what else I realised Alice? This bit really hurt."

He waited again, as if the sheer weight of his words became an effort.

"For nearly all of them I have already experienced the last time as well. It made me sad, very sad. The staff in the home of course just said I was silly and I should walk in the garden and get some air. Consider good things and think happy thoughts."

One nurse said, "Reflection is never a good thing, it is best left alone."

The man wiped his eyes. After another deep breath, he continued.

"Despite the dire warnings, I could not get the concept out of my head, Alice. How blindly we go through life, experiencing all these firsts. Then at some point, the table turns. You don't even notice. The 'lasts' start to invade your life. The 'firsts' become less and less."

The man cleared his throat. He waited. When he resumed his voice was husky and strained.

"In the garden by that huge willow, walking dutifully about as instructed, I thought of the answer. I wanted to tell somebody but who could I trust? So I kept to myself. The answer was of course ……. a special last time. I knew it had to be here."

The man looked about, smiling at the scene, gazing up at the sky.

" Remember when we sat here the first time. I loved you so much I couldn't speak. I suspect you saw my silence as being inspired by the view. Not so my dear. It was you. I could not believe I was here with you."

This became troubling for the old man.

For some minutes he sat hunched on the seat as the undergrowth about him settled and creaked in the morning sun.

"I stole the sandwiches from the staff fridge. They'll probably take all day to notice I'm not about. Then what will they do? Very little I suspect. By golly, I'd forgotten how steep those steps are to this place. Not that there's many of the steps left. Just crumbled away I suppose. Neglect. Our little world has moved on. Made the task that much more difficult. Still here I am."

Again the man lapsed into silence. He sat still and stared at the town and the gully. He loved every part of this place, this place they had made their home, their life together. Right down below in Maxime Crescent. The best house in the street.

He had averted his eyes as he passed by today, not wishing to see his life's work now an untidy rental property like all the others.

He seemed lost. As if his energy had run down. He looked at

his hands. They were still trembling from the exertion of the climb. He remembered when they were young and strong. Supple hands, capable of many things. A loving touch, the keyboard of a piano, the hug of their children, the making of their house, their work, their life. Now resting on his knees they had no purpose. What was left for them?
The man took one more lingering look at all about him then he leaned forward and put his face in his hands as if overwhelmed with the burden of his thoughts.
"Oh dear," he said quietly and sighed.

As minutes passed, his small figure became part of the landscape. Birds moved closer, creatures in the undergrowth resumed their tasks. The world breathed and the day warmed. Then slowly it hushed.

At some point the silence became noticeable.
The man lifted his tired head from his hands. He looked up. And his face beamed with happiness.
"Alice, you came," he said. "You remembered. I hoped but I wasn't sure if ...... Well, you know the situation."
Alice smiled. That same beguiling smile that had entranced him the first time and for many years thereafter.
"Of course I came," Alice said. "I couldn't have you sitting up here all alone. Talking to yourself. What would people think? It's our place Arthur. You and me. We're a team."

Alice paused. She looked so beautiful with the sun on her hair. Wearing that filmy dress he liked very much. Her eyes were so kind. Younger than he remembered.

She walked forward and sat beside the man, snuggling up close just like before. They sat together for a while enjoying this lovely moment.

Then Alice said, "It's our last time Arthur. You know that. We can't do this again. Ever."

She cradled the man's head on her shoulder.

"Oh my dear man," she said. "Oh, my dear, sweet man."

The man closed his eyes. He smiled a smile of utter contentment and his heart beat for the last time.

DIRECTIONS

It was a troublesome morning. Just one of those annoying days. (Although I feel I handle these things much better of late.) Our dog slipped out of the garden back gate and went wandering the neighbourhood. I took Mazy and Jojo to help in the hunt. They proved that children prefer fun to the task at hand.

Eventually, with Boz sulking in his kennel I decided to skip breakfast and eat on the road. Being your own boss allows these little freedoms.

I left as my wife decided to confiscate the childrens game tablets to allow them to concentrate on eating their food and communicating with her before school. She smiled an

exasperated goodbye.
(Perhaps I should have helped.)

Today's meeting in a dockside town down the coast would take place at 1pm. The drive was an hour. Plenty of time but I just wanted to be on my way.

I arrived at Shackleton a bit before 9am. More than a little intrigued as to what I might find. I had not been in this area for many years. (As you gain a degree of affluence your choices in leisure time tend to move upmarket.)
Once a busy port facility with rails and roads everywhere it is now a forgotten hero of the industrial age. And a trap for the unwary. There are many ways in and not so many ways out I had been told. A necessary road system in better days apparently.

My meeting concerned a possible resort complex on the southern edge of the place and the hope of finding investors. The town and its people were trying desperately to reinvent themselves after years of falling jobs, closures and lack of income. The initial impression was that the vision seemed to outstrip reality. I hoped the meeting would be cordial as I explained just what the planners were up against. Huge areas of derelict factory complexes, rotting warehouses. rail lines that went nowhere anymore. A tired run-down port area that had no appeal even as a curious relic. A main shopping zone with only half occupancy.

It was a sad, lost world living in its past. (I had done my research.)

I tried to garner some positives that I could sprinkle into the conversation. With no ships calling anymore the water on the few little beaches and in the river, I imagined would be clean and pleasant once more. Perhaps they could rebuild their wharves and introduce some deep-sea sports fishing. Nearly all the possibilities however, required funding, the one thing they did not have.

Resorts, sports fishing, golf courses, luxury or even good accommodation. Money, money, money.

I tried another train of thought.

Use what they have? Maybe they could reinvent the old glory days to their advantage. If the factory buildings were salvageable they could perhaps create an historic village or get some of the machinery working again and produce tourist items on the spot. Visitors love that stuff. See something actually made before their eyes and then buy it.

I stopped the car and sipped the remains of my drive-thru coffee. A meeting to advise on the likelihood of acquiring funding for a somewhat 'pie in the sky' resort. That was the extent of my supposed involvement. Why was I becoming concerned about alternatives for these townsfolk? Would they ask for or possibly even resent my input or ideas?

Of course, I had answered my own question. I was known for solving problems like these and on some occasions performing something akin to miracles. (The resort is a trap to get me involved.)

The car was sitting on a rise. Possibly in the remains of a little stopping place or lookout. Rotted and forgotten now. The last before the road descended towards the town. Shackleton occupied a giant dish of land with hills on three sides and sparkling ocean on the other. All the railyards and the factories were visible in the distance. They sat like a fat brown stain in the valley to the north of the main town area. For the first time, I noticed the hills around town. They were lush and green, the way the whole valley must have looked over one-hundred years ago. Nature was reclaiming its territory.
With little traffic about the town, it was quiet. Easy to imagine the way things were. Was there hope for this place yet? I mulled over the advantages and disadvantages of getting involved. Of saying 'yes' when they asked.
(I could hear my wife. "Oh God Simon, not another charity job. Don't get involved.")

Perhaps just a quick look. No harm in that. A brief wander through this derelict place to feel the past. The factory precinct was the goal.

The roads were hard to access. Several entries were closed
with dirt mounds or sealed off with concrete blocks and
the rail crossings were not passable. Was this an effort to
prevent vandalism or to save visitors coming to harm?
Then there was the river.
Eventually, by following a dirt road that skirted the back
of the whole area I arrived via a private passage past some
warehouses in the middle of the factories.
Truly a sad sight. Like trespassing in a foreign land. Some
great old names on the buildings. Dates announcing their
beginnings. Seemingly endless rusting lumps of giant
machinery with grass growing up around them. Sturdy
factory gates, all closed and chained. Many at odd angles.
I stopped in front of one substantial complex of buildings.

Walking to the entry with its small guard-house I could easily
see the workers making their way through the heavy gates
on up the roadway and into the big roll-back doors. Peering
through the guardhouse window. An old teacup with roses
and a pencil stub on the small table. Had the occupant left in
a hurry? There was no indication as to what they produced
once inside but obviously, they made a lot of something and
for some considerable time, it was very successful.
I squeezed through the quite grand old wrought iron gates
with the name worked into the top in a fancy scroll. What a
marvellous place. Now just silent except for a breeze gently
moving the grass and weeds causing pieces of tin roofing to

let out periodic squeaks. Closing my eyes I could hear once again the roar and rumble of industry. It was simply a matter of time.

Peering through a broken doorway of the giant building with its arched roof and skylights, the sun lit up a dim line of huge stamping machines, steam boilers, pipes and pulley-wheels, walkways and gangways all brown with rust and coated in fine dust. The salt air would not help. Could it be brought back to life? Would anything work or be repairable? They pressed steel here. Soldier's helmets to car bonnets to early house ceilings. Anything could be considered.

I stood at the doorway for some time imagining and wondering, then ventured in. Walking amongst the plant's assets it was so easy to hear the rumble of a day's production. Climbing to a metal gangway I could be that dirty, tough, muscular male with leather gloves hanging from the back pocket of his work pants, eyes squinting in the heat and smoke.

A group of pigeons took flight, up and out through the broken skylights. Why are there always pigeons in these places?

There were touches of humanity in hidden corners.

A threadbare cloth cap left where it had been forgotten and never retrieved. Some goggles with a cracked lens.

A paperback novel, 'Riders Of The Plains' complete with a serious cowboy on horseback staring from the cover.

Then one day they had all just walked away. The gate-keeper closed the gates, looked back one last time, sighed and left forever.

Outside at the gate in the silence of the empty day, I could close my eyes and feel the place as it was. The area was in essence, a theme park of history and industry. It needed to be realised. That would be the difficult part. Perhaps the impossible part. Could I convince a town and a whole selection of money men to commit to a very expensive dream of recreating the past. Should I be thinking such thoughts?
This strange empty landscape gave me some hope.
(If wishes were fishes we'd all cast nets in the sea.)

I walked about the roads and the buildings for over an hour. It was still only a little after 10:45am when I returned to my car. Nobody about. So strange. They shunned the place, these people of this town. With their world half empty there was logically no reason for taking a walk through a reminder of their misfortune.

I noticed him as I pulled away. A speck in the distance.
A flicker on the landscape. I was intrigued. There was somebody here after all. So I drove slowly, rolling the car along. As I drew closer he stopped, staring at the car as if it

were about to devour him. He stepped hastily from the road.
Well back into the grass and rough ground by a ruined fence.
As I trundled past I nodded but he just stared back.

Further on I slowed and stopped. I could see in the rear-
view mirror that he'd now continued trudging along the
road away from me. From the back, he looked old and care-
worn. But the man I'd seen was quite young. He had a brown
fedora pulled down on his head. A collarless striped shirt.
Dark trousers held up by braces. On his feet were some
sturdy black workboots. He was carrying a leather, box-like
case. I wondered if he was a local or was some eccentric just
passing through.
I watched him a little longer. The day was becoming
oppressively hot. Licked the sweat from my top lip. Poor guy.
I swung the car around and headed after him.

As I drew close, he heard the vehicle engine and once again
stepped well off the road.
Bringing the car to a halt I lowered the passenger window
and called out.
"This is a long road. Can I give you a ride?"

He sat next to me clutching his case on his lap. I had decided
not to ask him to put on a seatbelt. Something told me he
would not have liked that. It had taken a while just to coax
him into the car. Normally I do not pick up people in my

car. You never know who they might be or what they'd be capable of doing. Somehow this was an exception. It felt okay.

As we rolled away he seemed ill at ease staring partly at the landscape but also at the inside of the car. For some reason, I decided to continue driving slowly. Perhaps to give us more time.

"It's going to be a hot day. Best not to be walking eh."

He did not respond. I tried a different approach.

"My name is Simon. What's yours?"

He hesitated and then replied, in almost a whisper,

"Jasper. My name is ..... Jasper."

(Still those wild eyes. This man is troubled.)

"Well Jasper, good to meet you, I'll get you out of this area. Nothing much happening here anymore. I've got some time to spare so I can drop you off somewhere? Anywhere reasonable. You just name it."

He seemed to mull over my offer. Finally, staring straight ahead he said quite strongly,

"I shouldn't be here!"

(I noted a hint of desperation in his voice.)

It was almost amusing. Did he think he was trespassing? Was he lost? Was he just some strange soul who'd taken to the road? At least now I had a conversation.

"Well that's easy," I replied, trying to sound upbeat. "We all lose our way sometimes. Where should you be? I'll take you there."

(I waited, eyebrows raised in anticipation.)

"1923," he said softly.

MANIFESTO

I need to record these events. Guilt, shame, guile or unashamed opportunism. Don't judge until you hear the whole story. Life is not fair so life's participants should map their course accordingly.

It is eight months in. The course, 'Advanced Creative Writing' Degree is a two-year full-time commitment.
To mark the occasion, Adele Swann, with two n's, has invited her four best performing writers to read a totally new work to the rest of the students.
As course coordinator, she has set some guidelines. She wants something strong, outside basics, vibrant and

different, controversial even. It must be something to invoke thought and discussion from all who hear the work. It cannot be more than three-thousand words long. This last rule is to save the listeners from some of the more excessive detailing that can creep into work by her four favourites.

To my surprise, I am one of the chosen ones. By sheer coincidence I'm sure, two of the others are females. There is a tiny snigger as she reads out their names. Adele is a political animal and a female after all. Balancing genders would be part of the agenda.

She advises that Sonia Glubb (who badly needs a pseudonym) will be first, I will be second, Rachel Tarrant will be third and then Terry Masters will be fourth.

So confident is Adele of her student's talent that she has invited the Chancellor and a number of other University board members to the little gathering. Furthermore, she has spiced up the audience with senior representatives of quite a few major publishing houses. It will be held on a Friday.

It's called crescendo presenting. You build to a big climax. Sonia is a sweet young thing whose writing could best be described as cute. I am, according to Adele, a wise and clever observer of the human spirit. Rachel is a talented writer, obsessed with all things female. Her works are strong and balanced and almost never feature a male character. It's as if she has halved the gender of the human race.

Then there is Terry. God, I hate him. Actually, I don't.
He's a really nice guy. We hit it off. Friendly, helpful, good
to be around, always full of bonhomie and enthusiasm for
those near him. He is also massively talented. He just has a
way with words. He can throw together a paragraph that will
leave you gasping in admiration at its cleverness, connection
and ability to invoke ideas while being also involved in an
obscure mystic meaning from the first few lines.
He is destined to be a force in the literary world. He is
the only reason Adele has invited the assembly of literary
glitterati to our little show. If she leaves him too long he may
be discovered by some other party and she would not be
involved in the reflected glory.

When I first joined the ACW course I read some of Adele's
books. It was logical to gain a knowledge of the person who
would be in charge of my learning for the next two years.
I decided to keep my opinion to myself. Trust no one I
thought. Bland, poorly researched medieval melodramas.
She 'sells very well' other course people suggested. They
had all done their research and decided to keep their own
counsel.
I consoled myself by imagining that there was a place for
good average writing. No delusions here, I told myself. I will
never be great but maybe I can be very good. Better than
Adele I hoped.

Two days out. I have my laptop open reading through the final draft of my piece. I'm smiling quietly. It is really good. Well, I think it is. A bit over three thousand words but nobody will be counting and I'm reluctant to cut a single word. It all just works so well.

I have discovered that there are times when writing, that it is possible to read one's own work and be quite in awe of what is on the page. As if some other being has created the text and you have had no part in its birth. Yet there it is and you know that it is your work. This is one of those moments.

"Promise I won't look."

Terry Masters slides into the booth beside me. Already, Jake the coffee shop owner is working on Terry's favorite coffee and warming up a muffin for him. Some people are like that. Everybody remembers them and likes them and wants to do things for them. Terry just has to arrive and the process begins. No verbal communication required. It is not something he has encouraged or constructed it just happens.

I have to place my order with Jake every time I visit. Which is quite a lot. He does know my name now. That is a minor victory.

"You can look. Go ahead."

"No thanks. Where's the enjoyment in knowing what is coming. I want to be surprised, amazed and delighted on the day."

"I offer no guarantees."

Terry's coffee and muffin arrive with a beaming Jake smile. He tears the muffin in half and places one half in front of me. "World's biggest muffins. Orange and poppyseed. Nice but can't eat it all."

"So Terence." (Only I call him that.) "What form of genius do you have planned for our little soiree?"

Sipping his coffee he looks me over. Says nothing, keeps looking.

"What?"

"I have an idea," he says at last. "Bit radical but needs to be done. Should I be the one to do it? Why the hell not. Needs to be said. Long overdue. Get angry at times. Nobody will touch it. Don't you find that? The obvious is always the bit they leave out in polite conversations. The herd of elephants in the room so to speak."

"Not sure what you're talking about and worried that you appear not to have started it yet but I'm enthused by the word 'radical'. Let me guess. Sexual relations while climbing Everest? Freudian logic applied to teenage confusion? Charles Darwin as described by his monkey?"

Terry glances at me with that annoyingly charming smile.

"None of those, though I like that last one. Can I have it?"

"Sure, consider it a gift. Look whatever epic you're planning it will be yours to unveil and amaze us all. Adele has announced she will not be vetting any of the four works beforehand. In some grand gesture of faith and trust, she announced she believes all four of us will be so unique and wonderful that her knowledge of their content could put a 'stain' on the occasion."

"Stain?"

"It was in an email she sent to all the VIPs. I saw a copy of it." Terry leaned back and swigged the last of his coffee.

He shoved the remains of his portion of orange and poppyseed muffin in his mouth and said, enthusiastically, with crumbs asunder.

"My mind is made up. I know my subject, my plot and the many twists and convolutions that will lead my audience to the none too subtle climax."

"Another Master piece." (Terry was the butt of many jokes concerning his surname. It seemed rather immature to mention it.)

"Not for me to judge my friend. Who knows the moment until the moment is past?"

He looked about the little shop. Agitated, as if he was torn over his decision. Then he jumped up out of our booth. Stood looking down at me and my laptop.

"I'll bet what you've got there is damned good. You know, you really do have a future."

With this enigmatic uttering hanging in the air he was gone, complete with a friendly wave from Jake.

The proprietor then looked in my direction.

"Hey .... , you want another?"

The Terry factor was rubbing off on me and he'd used my name.

I saw Terry again. The night before the big event I invited him to dinner. On my tiny income from bar work and commercial cleaning, it was a generous gesture. He had told me once that he was sleeping in a spare room at his sister's house in the inner city. His sister's husband was a medical researcher of some description and they got on extremely well. (Naturally). His sister was a little put out that they spent so much time together, discussing whatever subject came to mind.
"I know sis' is a bit jealous but her husband is such an amiable chap and seems to be interested no matter what strange topic we choose to examine."

I chose Manglers, a strange hole in the wall place in an off the main road corner of some very old city terraces. It was run by Alphonso Mangle. The gossip had it that he was two generations removed from a liaison between a Chinese mother and a Turkish father. He had played Rugby and was quite good, with prospects but had given it all away to open his little restaurant because his real passion was cooking. My ongoing amazement was that Manglers had never been 'discovered'. It was so cheap. Perhaps it was the limited menu or that it was a little out of the way. I had found it by accident while walking home to my apartment from a late-night cleaning job. Alphonso was about to close. I was starving.

"I'll give you the scrapings of everything I have left for five bucks." he said.

It was a lot, it was delicious and he threw in some good red wine for free. In gratitude, I helped him clean up for the night.

Manglers only ever had three choices on the menu. Usually stews or casseroles but often some seriously exotic alternatives. You arrived and took your chances. Alphonso's devotees loved the food, the great wine and the man. Characters run good restaurants and he was a character. Everybody who went to Manglers kept it a secret. They told nobody, terrified that if Manglers became too popular it would be ruined in the process.

So I was breaking my rule.

Terry sat upright like a school-kid on best behaviour. His hands were clasped in front of him. From our rough wooden table, he surveyed the establishment from top to bottom as if recording the experience for posterity. He smiled benignly. He sipped the bottle of Cabernet Merlot and muttered, "Damn that's good."

Finally, he put his glass down and stared sternly into my eyes.

"Bastard."

When I said nothing he added.

"How long have you known about this place? Am I not your mate, a fellow starving wordperson? Do we not support each other in these times of almost endless crisis?"
"It's sort of an unspoken rule that you don't tell anybody."
Terry sipped the wine again.
"So I should feel honoured. You have gained me entry to this secret cabal."
"Yes."

Despite two bottles of the Cabernet Merlot and a fantastic beef bourguignon which seemed to contain another bottle of red I could not pry details of Terry's planned 'work' to be unleashed the next morning.
We parted, giggling like two brainless school-kids. Me to walk to my bed, Terry to grab a bus to his sister,s with her 'excellent' coffee-making skills.
For one vaguely sober moment, standing in the dark street, Terry took my hand and grasped my forearm with his other arm.
"Whatever happens tomorrow my friend, I want you to remember tonight as our last night of freedom. Nothing will ever be the same again. Let's meet here once a year on this very night, to compare notes and to talk of triumph."

As I walked unsteadily toward my abode I realised what the man had meant. Whatever he did tomorrow, I knew that it would be remarkable. The assembled book publishers would be fighting for his signature. I doubted I would see him again. He would be too busy to finish the degree. He didn't need it. I recalled pieces of some of his uplifting prose. The sort of work that made mere word junkies such as myself both envious and delighted. It gave us a measure, a goal at which to aim. He would be a darling of the critics. Not my words but those of Adele.

I was one of the early arrivals. Rajish (on the course to improve his written english rather than his storytelling) nodded to me as I entered and then nodded again toward the corner of the room.

A couple of the TV channels had sent along cameramen. "Glad it will be you up there, my boy. I would succumb to stage fright. Wonder if they'll consider all this worth putting to air."

"Perhaps if it's a slow news day," I suggested.

Adele was worried. All the guests were here. She fawned, she chatted, she worked the room.

"Where is Terry?" she queried, slightly wild-eyed, looking at me.

"Oh he'll make it," I said reassuringly, more worried about my part in the proceedings than whether the star had arrived.

Just as Adele, after holding on as long as possible, asked

everybody to be seated, Terry Masters appeared at the door
and took his seat next to Rachel. He grimaced at me.
"Got talking to my brother-in-law over coffee. Late to bed."
Adele at the podium looked reborn.

After a somewhat lengthy introductory address by Adele
in which she mentioned herself and her works on several
occasions, she extolled the exceptional talents of her current
26 students and their prospects in the literary world. It took
on the feel of a cattle auction as she suggested that certain
people in the audience would do well to obtain ownership of
these people at their earliest convenience.

Sonia Glubb surprised us all with a gritty piece that had
the audience intrigued. It concerned a girl, her boyfriend
and a broken down car in the bush late at night. It became
apparent that the boyfriend is mentally unstable. Her story
was building to a whole range of clever literary outcomes
when she chose a happy ending and the whole thing fell
rather flat. Polite but sustained applause because Sonia is a
nice girl.

My turn. Oh dear, have I chosen well?
I have a story about a boy who is the idol of his rich parents.
He is handsome, intelligent, liked and loved by all. In the
middle of the family building their luxurious new home
by the beach, the boy, their perfect child, is involved in

an accident that leaves him in a wheelchair. Suddenly he
is no longer a family asset, he is a burden. His mother
moves on and his father leaves him isolated in their near
finished beach house with only a housekeeper for company.
He knows that he is no longer valid. No longer able to
contribute to everybody's happiness. He finds a way to get
to the beach one day and wheels his chair into the surf. His
final act solves everybody's problem, including his. Silence
at the end. God, I think I see some tears. Then rapturous
applause. Wow. Even some pats on the back as I resume my
seat.

Rachel. Oh, Rachel. She is an angry young woman. I'm
sure she is straight. Some poor guy is going to marry her
someday. Become her project lap dog.
Her story is beautifully written. Two married women decide
one day they've had enough. They take off in a husband's
brand new sports car. It's a road trip. Roadside bars. A bit of
rough stuff where the males are made to look fools.
In fact one male is so angry he confronts them outside as
they leave. They mow him down with their car. Now they
are wanted by the police. A pursuit. Do they give in and go
back to suburban drudgery or possibly jail? They choose the
other path. They drive up into the mountains and straight off
a very high cliff.
Applause for the excellent quality of the writing and much
muttering about the plagiarism.

Adele reappears at the podium.

"Please forgive me for this interruption to proceedings but I cannot let this last writer appear before you without a few words regarding his work and his potential."

Adele is gushing, sycophantic and embarrassing. Terry it appears is a master (yes, she even used that tired cliche) of the modern written word. He is (apparently) her protege, a prodigy with almost unlimited potential. His use of language is unique, fluent, poetic and without equal in my opinion. You will all remember the day you first heard Terry Masters. As Terry passes my chair he whispers, "Should I walk up or fly?"

To the best of my ability to recall all that I heard, here is a reconstruction of Terry Masters' words that day. Some of my own recently acquired prejudices may have crept in but the essence of the narrative is unfiltered.

"Good morning everybody. I'm afraid my 'work' has gone a little over the 3000 word limit but I assure you all that the few extra sentences were vital in bringing this text to life, so please indulge me."

Adele nodded to the room reassuringly. Her smile perhaps a little silly.

"There was a young man named Terry who, in spite of the fact that he was in his mid-twenties, had not done a lot with his life. On a whim and because he had always enjoyed writing he managed after some effort, to obtain a position in an Advanced Writing course. His work in the course was very well received. It turns out he had a way of playing about with the language. The sort of playing about that sends critics and reviewers in their esoteric little world into a lather. Stuff that is hard work for people who just want to read well presented words in some logical sequence but adored by the literary elite. The same sort of people who giggle at their cleverness in doing a cryptic crossword while others are happy with the standard model."

Adele is looking a bit anxious.

"Faced with this new found burden of responsibility Terry decided to examine the road ahead. If a writer he was going to be then where was he going with this and what could he expect? Was this the path he wanted to be on as his life continued? If he was the new darling of the literati what was in it for him apart from a lot of glad-handing and guest appearances at pompous dinners. Terry did not want to live on bread alone. He desired caviar. So Terry did a little research. No, that's incorrect he did a lot of research. What he discovered quite surprised him."

(There was none of the Terry genius here. No urbane, witty flexions of the language. This was Terry talking about Terry.)

"Now friends," he continued, "here's what Terry discovered. 1. The publishing industry is just that, it's an industry.

Like other industries, they exist to make profits. They're not into philanthropy.

2. They don't publish books as such. They make a 'product'. And like any manufacturer, they want to shift as much of their product as they can.

3. Like all businesses, they're going to look for products that will appeal to the most people and thus produce the greatest sales and profits.

4. It doesn't take long to realise that a bloke who can twist words about to make them sing and dance so that they appeal to a tiny number of literary dilettantes is not a viable source for product. Selling a thousand products and being praised doesn't pay bills. It's all about volume.

5. So, my fellow class members. Here's the type of algorithm that publishers use when choosing their stable of authors.

a. Is the person famous? Go straight to a publishing deal. The book and the authoring is immaterial.

b. Is the person infamous? Same as above as long as the person isn't a paedophile.

c. Is the person already part of our inner circle. In the trade as it were. See 'a'.

d. Is the person exotic in some way? Ethnicity, background, knowledge, job etc? Worth a look.

e. Has somebody come to you with a jaw-droppingly good manuscript and will they sign a completely rotten one-sided contract because they are desperate to be published? Can we manipulate this to make it pay a lot? Worth a look if they can be brought to heel."

Adele is about to stand, to put a stop to this horror.
The Chancellor motions for her to remain seated.
Terry ploughed on his voice growing more strident.

"This starry-eyed young chap called Terry did a little more research on the course he is doing. He checked back to previous courses. He found that this prestigious course is fairly new. It has run three times over the last six years. How many of the eighty-two graduates of the ACW course have been taken up by one of our large publishing houses, for that matter, any publisher? Terry found that the number is four. Based on a night or two phoning around Terry found that of the seventy-eight other would-be authors who have not found a publisher, fifty-six of them have given up chasing their dreams and have stopped writing. The rest live in hope. Many enter various literary comps in some vague attempt to gain a little notoriety but they never win.
Now folks, our hero Terry was also intrigued by the fact that of all the ACW courses run or running, 82% of the participants are females. It goes without saying, good people, that the four past students chosen by publishers were all female.
Terry did more fact-checking and research. He found that of 'all' the books published in the last two years 79% of them were by females."

Terry Masters paused and raised his hands. (The Chancellor was enjoying the show immensely. Many of the students were taking notes.)

"Now let me tell you, our character Terry is a champion of women's rights. He loves women. He is in a relationship with one and sleeps with her often. However, the sad fact is .... the publishing industry is a female cabal. The managers, the publishers, the editors, all those people who matter and make decisions about who gets signed and who gets published .... they're all bloody women.
Also, if those few writers who are not yet disillusioned and are entering literary comps have not noticed by now. All the judges of these awards are women and all the winners are women and the winning stories are all about women.
To elaborate.
Terry decides that his talent is sufficient that he will seek recognition by becoming noticed. He will work hard at his craft and dash off lots of brilliant little two-thousand or three-thousand word short stories which he will enter in the many Short-Story Comps around the country. Winning and fame will follow. After all, they use 'blind' judging. No chance of cheating there. No chance the judges will know if you're male or female or where you're from.
Sorry friends. Yes, the first read is blind. Once they have the long list they troll through the names and addresses of

the authors and do their research. Guess what? The winner somehow miraculously is a local female who wrote a story about females.

Could this Terry guy in my story be correct? Look yonder good people, fellow students. Look at the senior representatives of eight major publishing houses sitting over there today, enjoying that nice chilled Chablis and the hors doeuvres. What's the common factor you see? Yep, all women."

Terry Masters squinted as he looked in the direction of the publisher's tables.

"I must correct that statement. There's one token male at the back. Looking a little out of place. Good day to you sir."

The room's atmosphere was becoming somewhat tense. Certainly the publisher's tables were a complete matching set of negative body language and scowling. Still, the Chancellor sat and waited for more. It was enough to stem a walkout. Terry continued.

"Somebody had to tell you all my fellow students. You're wasting your time. Everything is stacked against you. You're not going to get anywhere. Sure one or two of you might get picked up by some traditional publisher but you won't be famous and you won't make any money. The guy outside cleaning the floor will earn more than you. Best thing to do is get famous in some other field and then ask for a deal. Of course, you wouldn't be able to publish any fiction. It will be a ghost-written cook-book or children's picture book for you."

Terry leaned forward his hands squarely on the rostrum, his shoulders hunched.

"There's one final thing. Let's say our disillusioned hero decides to go down the self-publishing path. Go 'online'. You know, build it and they will come. Your book will finally be noticed and it's literary merit appreciated.
It won't be. They won't come. Go digital or POD and you'll be an outcast. You'll be an 'indie'. The vast traditional publisher's tentacles are long and their reach is far. You'll be ignored and shunned like some snotty gutter kid at a posh school. It's an elitist, snobbish, esoteric little world you're up against. You could have written the greatest work of the century, it will make no difference. You're lumped in with all the many thousands of dreadful pieces of crap fiction that have polluted our world via this medium. Apart from being buried and unseen, you'll be forever doomed. Like that tattoo you had done one drunken night, you'll be marked forever, damned as one of those who dared to go over to the dark side and out of the control of the traditional publishing empire. Reviewers won't touch an 'indie' book. Literary

competitions will just toss it aside once they notice its origins. Literary grants and other such funds will not let you in the door. The publishers, who control the bookshops, the printers, the reviewers, the marketing will see to that. You'll be a permanent outcast.

Some indie authors do alright you say.

Yes, they attend courses that teach you how to cheat the system by all the students creating fake reviews for each other and learning various other methods for fiddling the books. Is that really what you want?

In conclusion, our hero Terry has a life to be getting on with."

Terry stopped. He put his fingers together in front of his chest and bowed slightly.

"I thank you all for your patience, understanding and attentiveness throughout my talk. I hope I have presented my work clearly and given us all much to consider. There's probably more but I think you get the idea. To my fellow students and friends, especially the lads, I say, do what I am now going to do, stop wasting your time on a path to nowhere and find some other pursuit that will reward you rather than crush you."

With those final words, Terry picked up his notes, gave another slight bow with his head down then stepped away from the podium and walked straight out the door. The silence of his departure continued except for a nervous cough from somewhere at the back.

When it was obvious that Adele either wouldn't or couldn't move from her seat, the Chancellor stepped up to the microphone.

"Well, I must say that the last couple of hours have been most interesting and enlightening. I'm sure you'll all agree the four presenters have given us much to discuss and consider. This is, after all, a university. Where thoughts and ideas are let loose to roam through our minds. Please feel free to stay and enjoy the light refreshments."

He gave a non-committal academic smile and then also left the little auditorium.

The course did continue. I arrived the following Monday to find the doors were open and students quietly talking. Curiosity brought me back. Would Terry return? Well, of course he didn't. (About one-third of the students didn't ever come back.)

Adele arrived with a dour-looking old gentleman who she informed us would be running the course from now as she had 'other duties to attend to.' She looked grey. I felt sorry for her.

I stuck the course for several months. The dour old gentleman was an academic they had resuscitated.

His methods were academic and uninspiring. The course
became a history of literature.
News filtered through our ranks that Rachel had secured a
contract with Wheatherby-Mason.
A week later Sonia announced she was to have her book 'The
Goatgirl' published by Pendergast.
The news did not inspire me. The Terry talk was all coming
true. Most of the males had left the course.
Then I had a call from Millicent Courtney-Maze who asked
me to call her 'Millie.' Would I like to submit some of my
work for consideration by Gatewood Publishing? Did I by
any chance have a novel in the wings? Could we meet at her
office for a chat?

Almost a year has gone. I gave up the course not long after I
signed with Gatewood. I didn't have the time to write great
prose when I had a deadline for a novel about a dark journey
of four people captured by rebels in the Philippines.
Sonia Glubb has had success with her first novel though she
is called Sonia Garrett. I read it out of loyalty. It is sweet like
her. Childish like her. Not sure how she'll follow it up. Rachel
is about to release her first effort called 'The Journey', a look
at the early days of the female war.

I'm still working two jobs. My advance from Gatewood
was $2000, half of which I forfeited when I missed my first

deadline by two days. My 'minder' at Gatewood seems overwhelmed by her job or perhaps she just can't be bothered with me. It's hard to tell but there's no hand-holding. Nor any planned marketing budget.

After a number of attempts at finding Terry for a talk and perhaps a laugh, I have given up. I suspect he does not want to be found. He left his sister's house not long after the 'incident' and she does not know where he is to be located. She has promised to tell me if she hears from him. I called at his various haunts a few times by day and night and nobody knew anything of him or his whereabouts. Jake remembered me which was a tiny boost to my ego. Eventually, it all became too hard and I did not want to miss the second Gatewood deadline.

In a chance meeting with Rachel on the street, she seemed ambivalent about Terry.

"A lot of what he said was true," she espoused, "But hell, nobody wanted to hear it. Naive is what I'd call him. You've got to play the game."

I walked away from her promising to keep in touch though I knew we would not and considering the art of playing the 'game'. For most, you would not even be in the game.

I have one more longshot that I intend to fire regarding Terry. The drunken proclamation he made on the night of our visit to Manglers. Something along the lines of meeting once a year on the same date. That date approaches. Chances of such a grand gesture even being remembered let alone acted upon were slim at best but I was willing to test the theory. I was due to eat there again anyway. It had been near two weeks since my last visit.

I had plans. If I became a successful author I would find an obscure corner at Manglers and use it as my regular creative bolthole. The odd and varied personnel who made up the diners at such a place would be my inspiration, my assorted muses. Henri de Tolouse-Lautrec came to mind.

The night arrived. The twelve months had elapsed. I had met my second deadline with Gatewood and I was at peace. My minder had said, "Well done". High praise indeed from her and the editor had confided that the text was 'reading well' which could have meant anything from "this is a work of genius" through to "I can at least understand the basic premise".

I took a table in the corner where I could watch the door. My status at Manglers had grown from nice guy who once helped me wash the dishes late at night to 'man with a book deal', thus I was able to choose my table.

Timing was everything. The place was busy. Despite my new-found status on the pecking-order I doubted they would let me sit there all night and to explain my quest would sound rather silly. First, take my time with my order. In itself, rather lame as there were still only three items on the main menu any given night or day. Change my wine order. That was about it in the delaying tactics.

Mangler made moussaka that was a combination of bliss
and heart attack, it being so rich and creamy. The wine I
chose was a merlot. The man continued his knack of finding
brilliant wine that was still not crazy expensive.
The moussaka arrived and as I took my first mouthful
the wine was poured. God the moussaka was good. Hot,
flavousome, delicious. If I drank all the wine I'd have to walk
home drunk again. I had my wine glass to my mouth when I
realised there was a body obscuring my view of the door.
Trying to peer round the person a voice said, "Hullo mate,
it's good to see you again."

I confessed to Terry that it wasn't a coincidence that I
was here on this particular night. That I'd hoped he would
remember and show up. He then admitted the same thing.

So he found another chair and we sat in a happy twosome.
I concluded he really was glad to see me.
I learnt a lot that evening.
Terry had always wanted to be a journalist. His masterpiece
was to be an exposé of the whole publishing industry. He
sensed that it was corrupt or at least unscrupulous. So he
invented a name and managed to gain enrolment in the
university's prestige writing course.
"What? Hang on! Invented a name?"
"Yeah, sorry. My real name is Terry Bradshaw. Sis' was in on
it. Masters was our little joke."

As he progressed and did the course Terry spent all his spare time collecting data and details about how the industry worked. The more he discovered for his giant essay the more he realised how fraught, how false the whole publishing business had become. In the end, as he watched his ambitious fellow students following a path to ultimate failure he became annoyed. They stood no chance, the whole system was fixed. It was an insiders' club.

Maybe that speech at Adele's little get together was a mistake but he felt he had to do something.

"Hang on," I said, "what about the incredible work you produced while you were on the course? It was the main reason Adele even set up her tea party."

Terry looked abashed.

"Don't know what that was. Was never my intent to stand out. Tried to be invisible. Stream of consciousness stuff. I swear I just wrote down whatever came to my mind. I would read it afterwards and think it was nonsensical rubbish. I'd submit the draft expecting ridicule and people would say how much they loved it and how they found depth and hidden meanings. So I did more of the same. Perhaps your mind is at its best when it has no restrictions. Anyway I still maintain that stuff I produced would only appeal to a small audience and would be commercially unviable."

"The essay? The journalistic masterpiece?"

"Ah, missed that boat. Seems obvious now. I was presenting newspaper editors who I completely forgot, are in the 'publishing' industry and have book publisher connections, with a huge document which tore a lucrative section of their world apart. They all politely said no and I suspect put me on their industry-wide blacklist. Between my rant at Uni and my subsequent manifesto on the publishing industry I was and am 'not welcome' on their doorstep forever."

Terry's moussaka arrived along with the second bottle of wine he ordered. It was about now I noticed the man in front of me. This was not the rough, likeable larrikin I knew. The man with charity bin clothing and an endless lack of money. He was neat, tidy, well-groomed. He was wearing a suit!
A very nice suit. A shirt with french cuffs and understated gold cufflinks. His suit looked expensive. The watch wasn't a Rolex but it was something close.
I was leaning forward to pursue the reasons for this transformation when he asked me about myself. It's well-trodden psychological path. There's no more interesting subject for just about any human being than themselves.
I told him of the drop in class numbers, of the good fortunes of Sonia and Rachel and of my own writing project, working on the next bestseller. In the end, my curiosity won out over my ego and I stopped my personal, twelve-month diary trip for another question.
"Look, that's enough about me. Who is this transformed Terry I'm sitting down with? You sound the same but you are not the same ..... what's happened? Who are you now?"

Terry smiled and sipped his wine. He had an air about him.
Smooth.

"Old Mangler still knows how to find some top wine doesn't
he?"

"Terry!"

"Where would a wordsmith go when he's just slammed the
door on all the legitimate sources for his craft?"

"Please tell me. Where would he go?"

"Illegitimate of course."

"And that would be?"

He paused and smiled happily.

"Advertising, my friend. The one bloody place where they're
not judgmental, don't care about your past, your motives,
your sex life, your degrees or diplomas, whether you're
male, female or both, as long as you keep coming up with the
slogans and ideas. Write a good bit of selling copy for some
client's new product and you're hero of the month."

"Advertising?"

"You make it sound dirty. If you want real bottom rung of
existence you should check out the marketing people. They
make me realise that there are more horrible things to be
than dead."

"Ad-ver-tising?"

"Goop, sloop, doop. Gonna have a Choop."

"Yes, the most annoying combination of words to come out
of our language in a decade....... No, NO!"

"Yep, that was me. The client loves me. Its had some of

the best recall figures of any ad line in a 'decade.' They're shipping Choops out by the millions. Two new flavours in the wings."

"Okay Terry, I'm happy for you. Ethics aside, you're doing alright. I wouldn't have guessed."

Terry leaned across and tapped the table with his forefinger.

"I've done some sums, my prospective author mate. Took some figures left-over from my publishing workover. Comparisons. Selected two authors who've had success with best-sellers in the last year or so. Facts are hard to take but here it is, I've made more money in the last three months than they made out of their bestsellers over two years. Consider that my friend as you suffer the trials and lack of expensive lunches and put up with the putdowns at your publisher's office. Is it worth it? Are you enjoying the very minor acknowledgment of being a published author or would you just like to be financially stable and forget about being another face on page seven of Gatewood's long list of authors?"

"I'm not actually published yet. Still working on it."

Terry stopped, his glass halfway to his mouth.

"Then there's hope yet," taking a gulp of merlot.

'Out Of The Jungle' arrived in bookshops in the same week as Rachel's latest work. My book received some encouraging reviews. A couple of reviewers took the side of the rebel kidnappers and not my hero and heroine and another suggested it would be a good book to take on a long trip.

I did a strenuous round of interviews, signings, handshakings and interstate trips for which I was expected to pick up a lot of the tab. After several months my sales were flatlining. My first royalty payment was for $1889.00. The second was for $2011.00. The third $446.00. They never rose above that last figure again.

Gatewood said they were disappointed and had expected more. They were in two minds about doing an international release. There was still a slim chance of somebody buying the movie rights. Would I like to submit a finished manuscript for another book? They could not offer me any advance.

Rachel's book, 'The Sister's Secret' was about a group of girls in a private girls school who called themselves 'The Sisters.' It was nasty and involved the girls luring boys to the school cellar and murdering them. It became a runaway best-seller.

I met Terry at Manglers a year later. The best I could do in between was the occasional coffee with the man. He was always 'busy'. Gatewood were 'considering' my final draft for book two. He insisted paying for everything.

"You don't look rich," he said.

He still did.

"I don't get it," I said to him, "Rachel has put out two more books. She's prolific. How does she do it? They're those big

airport jobs with her name in 300 point type on the front."
Terry looked at me with disdain.

"How dumb can you get my friend? They're factory books!
Rachel is now a product. She doesn't write the books. She'd
be fully involved in marketing. At best she'd give them an
outline of a story. They have a team of writers who churn out
the text. Bit like a sausage factory conveyor belt. Hence the
name. Don't think you're ever going to achieve that status.
You're a white male and not the least bit exotic. Women buy
over three times as many books as men. You figure it out."
I sat poking at my fabada asturiana. I hated Terry as much
as I did at the writer's course. Because he was right. He was
always right.

Time passed.
As I walked in through those large ornate doors (possibly
too ornate) of Maris Pullman, Lindy smiled that smile that
warmed my heart. She was so nice, so welcoming. Which
is why she was on the front desk. Everything at the agency
was planned and in place for a reason. From the moment
our clients walked in they were being manipulated and
controlled.

"Morning Sir," she said with that slightly husky, caramel-
coated, whipped cream voice. "Another new suit I see?
You're looking good today."

"So are you Lindy," I said, "So are you."

On the sixth floor, in my office overlooking the harbour, a large mug of exceptionally good, hot coffee (with just a drop of bourbon) was sitting on my desk. (Lindy always rang upstairs to alert them that I was in the building.)

As I lay back in the particularly soft leather of my chair I swung round and watched the ferries way down below at the wharves and all the little people moving to and from their little jobs.

"Excuse me, sir."

It was Jacki, my PA. Slim, beautiful and quite bright. She was leaning round the door of my office smiling across the expanse of plush carpet and that persian tribal rug I had decided I liked when suggesting the fitout.

"Terry said can you spare a few minutes in the screening room to go over the Warren's campaign draft? Some the wording needs refining."

Terry's office was at the other end of the long hallway that skirted the atrium. A bit like being on the bridge of an ocean liner.

As the crack creative team at MP we occupied the whole floor. Of course we could just get each other on the house phone but then we wouldn't have been able to watch the girls heading up and down the hallway.

As I walked out past Jacki's desk I noticed a book sitting next to her phone. Rachel Tarrant it screamed from the cover. Jacki saw me looking.

"It's her new one," she said, "I just adore her work. So clever.

How does she do it. She must be very rich."

I looked at Jaqui. Sweet adorable Jaqui. I planned to sleep with her very soon.

"Perhaps not as much as you think," I replied and moved off to meet Terry in the screening room. In this shallow world nobody ever drowned.

(Note: My second book was described by several critics as a work of particular literary merit.

'An august leap of erudition, displaying an exceptional use of word power and a splendid sweep of ideas and structures so as to leave the reader in a swoon at the audacity and experimental powers of the creator.'

It was about a man who misplaced his soul. The whole book concerned his fruitless search about his house for this missing item. He was not certain where he had left it but was vaguely sure it was still on the premises.

The critics loved it. They fawned and praised and just when their pens seemed destined to run out of superlatives they added, one and all, that of course this work was very 'esoteric' in its nature and thus would have limited appeal. They knew the market. It sank without a trace and Gatewood decided they would no longer be publishing my work.)

Terry was right.

JABLANAC

There is the moment. It creeps about the room, stalking
you in a cat-mouse motion until it breaks through from the
sub-conscious to the frontal lobe. Then you are aware of its
presence.
The song got to me. Music does that. It's an individual thing.
Everybody has their trigger. A moment, a sample, some
fleeting flicker of audio that turns on a memory.

I was idle. Sitting at my desk in the back of our house.
An early morning, Springtime sun streaming in the window.
The house was quiet with late sleepers upstairs, yet to
appear. Tapping a pen on the desk pad, trying to remember

the note I was about to write. Idle and content.

It stole into my consciousness like a thief in a darkened alley. An echo of other days. For a few seconds I lifted and turned my head to listen. The airy brightness of it. A huge blue sky came to mind. Soaring strings and vocals that spoke of all that quick part of life when you have it all and know nothing of the consequences. It is a gift that is only recognised when the gift has gone and you wish with all your heart that it could be given one more time.

Then I was there, with her, standing beside a secondary road, in the sun, on a high point of the coast. White glaring rocks and white stone hills behind and a glaring blue ocean away in the distance.

Nobody else in our world at that moment. An empty, still landscape stretching away in all directions.

"Midsummer on Mars," I think I said to her.

The light hurt our eyes. Nothing green existed. Just the rocks and the light.

It's where the guy had dropped us. Next to a signpost at an artistic angle. He'd mimed some need to go away inland and this was as far as he could take us.

We wanted to sit down. There were suitable rocks next to the road. But by standing with your eyes closed you could drink in this time and space and store it in your soul. I looked and the girl also had her eyes closed. Of course, we knew nothing of growing older and losing these threads of existence.

It was just another day. Of no particular importance.

A happy journey. The freedom, youth and the possibilities.

The sadness and the realisation that these things have an

end, that would all come later.

It was a nothingness in a fraction of a day on a trip to

somewhere else. Who can say why we randomly select tiny

pieces of past events and mark them for ongoing reference

and regret?

God 1968 was a wonderful time to be alive.

I'd met her a week before in a youth hostel in Trieste. She

was travelling with another girl. We had talked in that vague

flippant way that was all about appearing carefree and

wanting nothing. Her friend complained. It was her raison

d'etre. The food, the country, the people. She liked nothing.

The question that nobody in this little group of strangers

was willing to ask is, "Why?"

"Why are you here at all? If this whole journey is for you a

terrible burden, then give up, retreat to your bland existence

in some comfortable suburb, in some quiet, safe part of

the world and live out your life without any hint of foreign

nastiness."

I watched the girl as her friend complained. She was

unremarkable yet pretty. Short cropped hair. A tomboy in

girl's shorts, thick socks and hike boots. They seemed to

make her light frame, her brown legs even more appealing.

Most of all I enjoyed her quirky acceptance of all things about her. Was she naive or just a forgiving? In 1968 everybody was making an effort to be particularly 'nice.' 'Love' was the overused word of the time.

We all talked about where we were headed. After five days wandering the streets of Trieste, there were ten of us who all wanted to be on our various ways. Five sets of twos who after this day would probably never see each other again. That was the way it was.

Overnight, Conroy, my American buddy and travelling companion whom I'd known since working together in a London bar, called home. He did this periodically to reassure his parents that he was still alive and all was well. Except that it was not. His brother had been in a car that hit a truck outside a gas station near the eastern turnpike upramp.

He was needed home immediately, to sit by the bed of his comatosed brother and hold his hand.

Apologies and a good deal of hand-shaking and best wishes saw him gone in the night.

In the morning I lay in bed longer as the others in the bunk room all packed and left.

I could go on alone. It would be okay? Despite all the bravado, even the young are afraid of loneliness. By the time I'd dressed and headed for the dining area I had given up. Back to London. Work another year selling booze to annoying drunks. Find another travel companion and head off again in the summer.

Here is where it would end for now.
However, occasionally some magic drops into our lives.
At the time we barely recognise its presence. Just a series
of events that click into place. On this morning there must
have been several audible clicks but in my self-pitying mood,
I missed them all.
The dining room was all but deserted. Some German guys
all studying a map and the girls from last night, in earnest
discussion.
While I ate cheese and bread and drank milky coffee I stared
out the windows at the people of Trieste. I consoled myself
with the knowledge that I had engorged their country from
the boot heel all the way up. Literally and geographically.
The Amalfi Coast, Rome, Venice, Florence, Napoli, Pompeii
and Herculaneum and a lot more. I could tick off Italy for
now. At twenty-two you assume there will always be another
time. Endless returns are possible. The coast of Dalmatia,
Greece, Turkey and who knows where else. They would have
to wait. Time and its passing had no relevance.
Back at the girl's table, I noticed that Sandra the complainer
had gone and her friend was sitting alone and appeared to
be tearful.
The Magic had begun.

The signpost on the edge of the road pointed down a

steep unsealed side road. A road in need of repair. It said
'Jablanac'.
"What do you think?" I said to her.
We consulted our Michelin map. It seemed we were a
long way from anywhere. In a desert of rock with no great
incentive to create habitation when more fertile land lay
elsewhere.
She turned from the map and looked at me with those lovely
brown eyes.
"There hasn't been another car since he dropped us off. And
when they come they're reluctant to pick up. I say let's have
a look at Jablanac."
Then she smiled that lovely secretive smile.

As we walked through the ongoing white stone desert,
down the steep road that kept turning back on itself to the
unknown that was Jablanac, we amused ourselves with
concocted stories of devil worshipers and satanic rituals
involving unwary travellers.
Picturing my travel companion naked, lying on an altar
by the light of numerous candles was not an altogether
unpleasant concept. Our first night together had been in the
dormitory of the University of Rijeka. Some friendly students
had offered us food and accommodation. Something never
refused when travelling on a very limited budget. The girls
slept in a separate dormitory.
While our relationship on this journey had not been

discussed I had certain hopes that it could lead beyond mutual companionship.

After Sandra's abrupt departure, to return to the bosom of her family my new partner had presented a sad figure sitting alone in the dining room. My enquiry and the subsequent story brought forth within me a moment of almost spiritual relief.

Despite my breathless enthusiasm to take immediate advantage of this God-given opportunity I broached the possibility of us teaming up with what I considered a great deal of delicacy and aplomb.

She readily and I thought enthusiastically agreed.

On yet another curve in the road, a break appeared in the monotony. Between the washed-out pale blue of the sky and the white rock, landscape appeared the dark blue of the Adriatic. Ahead there were trees and greenery.

Our enthusiasm for the delights of Jablanac was renewed.

As we sweated round yet another turn a small car rounded the bend behind us. We skipped aside. The car made a rather strangled beep sound and a hand waved as it disappeared on down the hill.

"Couldn't he see we were dying here?" I asked.

She always had an answer.

"C'mon, I'll race you to the bottom."

The town was small. Sturdy buildings made of the local

stone. A few streets and a tidy harbour with an expansive open area to the walled drop and the water. It was pretty, while being stark and alien. We sat beside the water, tired, sweaty, dirty. Our backpacks thrown down beside us.

Then another little moment occurred. A large woman with an apron over her dress and a dark green scarf round her weathered face, walked up to us. She had a water pitcher and a glass. She smiled, placed the items next to us and said, in rounded Slavic tones, "Drink. Yoou d-rink."

We watched as she walked back and disappeared into a doorway opposite. Then we emptied the water pitcher, handing the glass back and forth. The water appeared pure. So the satanic rituals were not about to happen.

When we returned the pitcher the woman blushed and offered us more. We drank again and filled our water bottles.

"Shop?" we asked. Then acted out the process of shopping. She caught on, directing us to a building that said 'POSTA' on the front.

It was the shop of many items from groceries to shovels as well as postage.

Inside we bought two cans of some type of stew, based on the picture on the label, then added a bottle of brandy. It was our first experience of the low subsidised prices of a communist state. The local alcohol was exceptionally cheap. A clever way of keeping the populace endlessly happy?

"No .... no," the lady in the shop had said apologetically when we asked about accommodation.

"Looks like a night in the hills," I said outside, "I don't think they get many visitors here."

My companion smiled a benign smile that told me nothing then said, "I want a swim first."

We found a path around the cliffs away from the town. There it was just below us. The warm welcoming crystal waters of the Adriatic Sea.

"This will do. There's virtually nobody about. This place is almost a ghost town."

"Sure, okay," I replied.

Yes, of course, I was intrigued. What was about to happen? Jump in with our shorts and shirts, strip naked? All these options. I hung back as my sweet companion peeled her boots and socks from her perfectly proportioned feet. I fiddled with my laces as she slid her shorts down to reveal a tiny pair of white knickers. Then she stood up straight and arching her back she reached down to the edges of her t-shirt and slid the garment over her head. No undergarment appeared. Just two beautiful small but perfect breasts. Without a backward glance she hopped down from the path and slid, ever so gently into the water.

My little silver fish swam a few strokes from the shore then turned and called, "C'mon speedy, the water's fine."

I had the ongoing task of removing the remainder of my clothes and hiding my erection under a dark blue pair of

Marks & Spencers briefs.

As the lights came on around the town we lay together on our elbows facing out the front of my tent. We were on a grassy little platform near the treeline above the town. It was a type of pine forest.

"I'm pretty sure they don't have bears in these parts," I'd remarked as a way of being witty then in the back of my mind I wondered if in fact they did.

I was proud of my tent even if a little guilty. Somewhere between the Netherlands and Germany I had lost my cheap British pup tent. In a sports/outdoor store in Cologne I had stood looking at replacements horrified at the prices. My American Buddy took me over to a rather deluxe two-man tent and said, "Listen man, I'm gonna buy this baby for both of us. I hate that little piece of crap I've got and I hate sleeping alone. And no I'm not queer or nuthin."

He had plenty of money. Americans always do. I tried to thank him. I could spot a charitable gesture even then but he was magnanimous and would hear none of it.

When he departed to be with his brother he handed all his gear to me.

"Hey man, take it and damn well use it. This gear's no good to me. I can't take it on the plane."

We'd cooked our nice tins of strange stew on the American's dandy little pressure stove. Now we just lay content on our stomachs and drank brandy.

While I did my very best impression of a cool young guy in charge of the moment my mind raced ahead in what could best be described as a hearty mix of fear, anticipation, hope and helplessness.

I wasn't a virgin but I was no master of the art of seduction either. My experience all hung around bumbling drunken efforts and one brief moment when I was taken in hand by a mate's sister back home.

The swimming incident further enhanced my opinion that the girl next to me was a bit further down the path of sexual adulthood.

As the last light slid away over the sea she turned and rolled onto her back. She picked up our brandy bottle and exclaimed, "Wow, it's half empty. We must be drunk." Then she looked at me. I leaned over her a little.

"Oh, this is awkward," she mumbled.

Hell, I thought. She doesn't like me, she's a lesbian, she's saving herself for another.

"Are you going to try to kiss me?" Her voice was slurred.

Would the brandy help or hinder?

I decided to be honest.

"Well, yes ......"

She paused. Here it comes I thought. The can we just be friends speech.

"Okay. When you said you wanted to team up I was a little scared. I knew this would happen. Truth is, I've only had sex once before. I'm not an expert. Please don't laugh. I know how it is with guys. Been there, done it. Can you be kind and show me? I'll do anything you want. Just be patient."

The next morning we left our tent. Zipped it up and with just our towels we walked down the hill into the town. We had bowls of muddy coffee in the shop, bought some cake and hand in hand walked round the path to the south of the town to the Zavratnica Inlet. It was deserted.

We swam, we lay in the sun, we explored the skeletal remains of a WWII ship at the bottom of the inlet. Most of all we held each other in and out of the water and kissed and touched. For this day and the next, time had stopped. There was only the two of us.

At night I taught her all I knew about sex. I don't think she suspected my limitations. We just wanted to hold and be held. Skin on skin. It was that once in a lifetime happening when one human discovers the unimagined joy of being completely given over to another and the feeling being wholeheartedly reciprocated.

Sitting by the wharf on the third morning we noticed a white sheet hanging from an upper window of one of the stone buildings. There was a dark mark in its centre.

"Not too good at washing," I remarked in my worldly way.

She looked abashed. Bowed her head.

"I know what that means," she said quietly. "When these

people marry they are keen to demonstrate that the new wife is a virgin. That mark is blood."

I was caught. What to say. I decided on humour.

"Or the groom takes a small bottle of pig's blood with him to the bedroom. I mean who's to know?"

She laughed. All was well.

With my arm around her waist, her head resting on my shoulder, little coloured wooden boats shifting about on the harbour tide, the world could not have been a better place. That's when I heard it. Coming from one of the waterfront houses. So incongruous in our surroundings. A guitar, strings, gentle words. A simple western world ballad.

"I love this song," she said.

So did I. At that moment it was truly beautiful.

Something touched my shoulder.

It was Alex, my youngest child, already dressed.

"Where were you Dad? Miles away somewhere?"

He looked round from my back, his face in mine.

"Hey, I'm going over to Mark's house. Gonna swim in his pool."

"Our's not good enough?"

"Mark's is a lot bigger. Water polo and all that stuff."

"Be careful on your bike and don't drown."

He looked back from the door.

"Dammit Dad I was planning to be stupid in the traffic and then drown myself. You spoil all my fun."

I watched him riding down our driveway and along the street.

He was a funny kid. I wondered if he knew how much I loved him.

We left Jablanac the next morning. A little way up the hill a woman stopped and gave us a lift. Perhaps after being seen about town we were considered safe. She took us quite way south. In Split we excused ourselves early from a pension dinner to fall onto the bed and feel our bodies together. I could not stop. I wanted to own her, to devour her.

In Dubrovnik an old lady rented us a room for two days. We wandered through this wondrous walled town but kept returning to our little room be with each other again.

"I'm getting sore she told me in the afternoon of the second day but it's okay I don't want to stop."

In an act of immense self-sacrifice, I announced that the next day would be sex free. It would do us both good.

She queried my sincerity when we spent all day in a bus crawling over the mountains on the way to Skopje and then waited in the station platform for a late train to Thessaloniki.

Camping was not an option in Thessaloniki so we booked into a hostel with separate male and female bunkrooms and an officious man and woman who kept them that way.

I kissed her often in the streets and ran my hands over her body.

We sold our blood at the hospital to supplement our

dwindling funds. Her blood was type 0. Mine was relatively
rare and commanded a good price. Overcome with lust
and emotion I returned to the hospital alone two days later
and made a deal with a man whose mother was to have an
operation and I had the blood he needed. He needed quite a
lot.
It was my plan to take her out to a fine dinner and proclaim
my love for her. Instead, I spent two days laying about
eating slowly trying to regain my strength and being told by
numerous regular donors that I had pushed my luck quite
considerably.

When I recovered sufficiently we hitchhiked out of town
with the express purpose of finding somewhere to resume
our lust. We rutted like two insane goats in a pine forest.
Dripping with sweat, hot exhausted and giggling like naughty
children we kept up all morning and into the afternoon
taking turns to be on top, our fingers locked together.
Still, I had not said the 'love' word. The situation had to be
right. Perhaps she would be first. Who could say?

In Kavala we stayed in a room above a bar. They played loud
Greek music till 1am every night. We found ways to work in
time with the beat. Greek music is surprisingly stimulating.
Outside Alexandropoulos we camped in a field. Idling time
away by a small stream we talked about many things. We
were so in tune. Words were easy. We were building each

other's lives. Piece by piece. All of these days being stored away.

It was a particularly nice field but the owner of the field discovered us after two days and told us to move on.

Just over the Turkish border and having little luck with cars we decided to try the standard hitchhiker's trick of 'one lone girl' while her companion hides until the ride is snared.

A giant tourist coach stopped. Once the door was opened I emerged and joined her climbing on board. The young driver laughed.

"I would have taken you both," he said. "Make yourselves at home. All the way to Istanbul. I'll even drop you at the American hostel."

The bus was empty. We stretched out at the back and slept through parts of the journey, still holding hands.

The driver played music, mostly western. He even played that song.

Once again in separate dormitories, I waited till the morning to see her again.

When I went into the dining room she was there, in the middle of a large group of all nationalities. She gave me a wave. I was introduced around the table. Everybody was young and life was just great. Adventures and plans abounded. We laughed a lot.

On the second day in Istanbul we had been to the Topkapi Palace and wandered in awe through the massive Blue Mosque.

On the third day, she was once again in the dining room before me. She was sitting with two young guys. God, she looked delightful. That lithe young body in her shorts and t-shirt. I was introduced to two companions. Both English and very well-spoken.

"Let's find the Grand Bazaar," I suggested to her, "we might come across some bargains."

The British guys were enthusiastic. For a moment I thought they intended to join us but they had been to the bazaar many times. They gave us some bargaining tips.

When we entered the cavernous wonderland I had a plan. I would find a shop with rings. Any rings. I would buy her a ring and then outside the shop I would tell her it was a token of our love.

After looking at numerous carpets, lots of brassware, meerschaum pipes and cigarette holders, elaborate hookahs, spices and herbs we came upon a trinket shop selling rings and bangles.

"I'll buy you a ring," I said. "Go on, choose one."

She looked pleased and settled on a nice little, inexpensive silver item. To disguise my motives I bought myself a puzzle ring.

We walked for a while gazing at the endless array of exotica on offer then stopped to try some Turkish coffee. The sweet muddy brew that the locals sip all day.

"That ring," I said, "it's a token. Till I can get something better. A token of our love. When we head back to Greece it will be something to hold onto. A sort of first step for us." There, I'd said it.

She looked startled. Put down her coffee. Her fingers moved to her hand and she looked at the ring. She stayed silent for a while. Was she overwhelmed by my declaration or was there something I was missing?

"Oh, I had no idea. I thought you were just being nice."

"I was ..... being nice. I don't understand. Is something wrong? I love you."

She looked me in the eyes.

"And I love you. You're wonderful. So sweet, so nice. And you saved me back in Trieste when I was stuck. But I haven't finished seeing the world yet. Those two British guys are heading for Iran, maybe even Afghanistan. You can come if you like."

I was temporarily speechless. She 'loved' me but in a non-committal, general sort of way. Now I was no longer needed?

"Are you crazy? I've heard stories. Once you get past here the rest of Turkey and those other places, they're not safe. Robberies, murder, disappearances, rape. How do you know those two Brits won't rape you?"

She laughed.

"Because they're homosexuals. They're really nice. I'm

swearing off sex for a while."

We talked for some time but quite early I realised the affair was over, if there had ever been an affair. In two days she would be heading east out of Istanbul and I would be alone. I briefly considered tagging along but I'd heard too many bad things about where they planned to go. There was something else she said that day, as we ordered another coffee and chatted, while I tried to appear brave. I asked what particular contraceptive she was taking.

"Oh I don't bother with that," she said, "fate will decide things. Your body knows. If you don't want to have baby, your body won't allow it. Just have to use your mind but you need to say it with Sandalwood incense burning. That's why I always carry some."

Her preventative measures consisted of sniffing sandalwood scent? My God?

I looked into her sweet, adorable brown eyes as she extolled this hippy rubbish and realised that the girl sitting opposite me, cupping her coffee cup to her lips contained enough of my sperm to give birth to a small army.

Back in Thessaloniki I sold my blood once more for a wad of US dollars and celebrated by having several different bowls of cold pudding in a local shop near the hostel.

Three guys in a van offered me a place in their combi and we spent the next two months having a great time, getting drunk and wandering Europe.

Occasionally I'd hear that song again and there would be a
wrench of pain and sadness. I think I really did love her but
youth is an excellent balm that heals emotional issues quite
quickly.

For years I wondered what became of her. Did she make it
round the world and see all she wanted to see? Did she come
through unscathed? Or, did she discover, some months after
our parting that she was indeed with child and did she give
birth somewhere to our son or daughter?
To this day the sound of a front doorbell makes me a little
nervy. Some lost soul in search of their father.

Well, the song is finished. I hear my wife in the kitchen at the
espresso machine. It is Sunday and appropriately the sun is
continuing to shine on a warm, clear, restful day.
My secret remains intact and it is good to be alive.

BACKTRACK

A man on a street corner. Hovering between movement and reconnaissance.

"God," he thought, "nothing has changed."

He stood where the taxi had left him. On the main street near the stock and station agent. 'Bulmers' it said in gold letters across the top of the window. About eight cards on display. Each with pictures and some statistics about why this particular holding was the property for you. 'Most fields sown to pasture', 'two silos', 'good water from a creek and three dams', 'substantial outbuildings and barn', 'magnificent homestead with large kitchen'. Another large sign with sheet tacked on the front listed the date of the next stock sale and

the expected beasts that would be on offer in the yards.
Frank Bulmer was about the same age as his Dad. His sons
must now run the business. He'd been to school with one of
the Bulmer boys. Could not recall his name.
He became alert. Keep moving. Little place like this,
everything and everybody is noticed. Especially if dropped
by taxi. It meant you'd come from Chalby, probably from the
airport there. You were somebody of interest. It's why he'd
stopped the taxi round the corner.
The trip had been in silence. Chalby people are like that.
Reserved, quiet or just bored? It allowed some time to look
about. Take in any changes. There appeared to be none of
any consequence though the town looked fresher, better
maintained than he remembered.
Street furniture in keeping with the heritage order and the
trees along each side were much bigger. Of course, they
would be.

He moved off casually, still in awe of the familiarity he felt.
Using a backpack instead of a suitcase had been a last-
minute idea. Even here there must be enough of them to
become unremarkable. Though upon reflection he was a
little old to be part of that backpacker scene.
With his beard and his hat he hoped he remained
inconspicuous.

It was 4pm. The funeral was tomorrow. Pray the motel is still there. Staying at the pub would be too exposed.

"Hey fellas, you'll never guess who's back in town?"

"Thought he was too good."

"Broke his old man's heart."

"Never forgive him for that."

"He was such a nice kid. Wonder why he went and did what he did?"

The newsagency, Roly's outfitters, the saddlery. Like yesterday packaged and rolled out before him. Perhaps they were all a little less shabby. His memories of the town were that it was worn down on its heels. Exhausted. It seemed to sparkle now. Clean, fresh with a polish that belied its past. Lots of nice street furniture and trees. Was it always so? Now the moment. He didn't want to look. He felt a cold shiver run down his back. Closed his eyes for a second. The doors were painted black. They had been dark green. The stonework around the entrance was unchanged. The sign still hung above his head on its wrought-iron beam. 'WHYTES' is all it said, all it had ever said. There was never any need of a tagline or slogan. Everybody knew Whytes. A sheet of paper was pinned to the door. It said simply, 'Closed due to bereavement.' Rather an understatement. The owner was dead. The business was no more. Then it all became overwhelming. Removing his hat the man leant his forehead against the big doors. He shuddered. He had not anticipated crying but tears ran down his cheeks.

He fingered the grain in the stout wood, waiting until he could hold a breath then said, "I am so sorry Dad. This is not how I wanted it to be. Forgive me for that at least."
Standing back the man glanced about. Nobody watching. He added, in a whisper. If you'd just told me. I could have made it. Somehow I'd have fixed it so I could have made it. Did you think .... I know, things were said, things you can't take back .... but did you think I wouldn't come? Is that why you were afraid to ask?"
The man's throat is now aching. He touches the door once more as if it is a holy relic.
Finally, he adds, "We were friends again."
He replaces his hat and moves on, trying to breath normally, sniffing. He wipes his face with his sleeve as a man and woman pass by glancing at his distress.
Speeding up he proceeds, head down, until he is in the forecourt of the only supplier of petrol and diesel in the town. A monopoly that did not endear the owner to his patrons. Chalby was just far enough away to make driving to their better prices not practical. Though some still did it in protest.
Something new! The old fuel pumps are much more up to date.
And there, across somebody's gardens full of vegetables, on the road out of town, is the same red and yellow fluorescent sign that spells out 'Maxi's Motel.' 'Best Rooms in Town.'
A distant light in the old darkness of his youth.

He remembers the sign as always sputtering with parts blacked out but this evening it is fully functioning. Bright and cheerful in its welcoming neon glow.

The woman at the desk is reading. Engrossed in her novel she only looks up at the last moment and smiles.
"Do you have a room?"
She smiles again.
"Oh we always have rooms, dear."
She looks at his notations on the register.
"Well, welcome, Toby Whyte." Did she hesitate when she said his name?
"How long will you be staying?"
"Oh, just for tonight. I'll be on my way tomorrow."
"Food?"
Once again she hesitates and smiles benignly. He might be able to get something at the pub or she can have soup and sandwiches sent to his room. He chooses the latter.

He does not sleep well. The bed is fine. Too many demons haunt the night. Then at dawn, there is that last period of peace and slumber. When he wakes it is late. The suit hung for the night has lost most of its wrinkles. No time to eat and no real hunger. Just a glass of water.

Yes, of course he can check out later.
"I should be back by 1pm."

She reaches over the motel counter and takes his hands in
hers.

"It's so good to see you back Toby. Everybody is waiting. I'll
be thinking of you. Good luck." That smile again.

"Good luck?" he whispered, outside and on his way.

With insufficient deaths in the area, it is the Meeting Hall
that says the town's final goodbyes. As he walks up the main
street there are others who seem to be headed in the same
direction. It is understandable. His Dad ran the tiny 'Whytes'
cafe all his life. He would be well known.

What was the woman in the motel talking about?

More people gathering, walking near him and with him.

No words.

There is a crowd outside the hall. A very big crowd. A crowd
who all fall silent as he approaches.

Oh God, this is the loathing and hatred he was expecting.

Still the volume of the crowd is surprising.

They part as he reaches them. Hats off, heads all bowed
respectfully. Many mutter his name and say words of
comfort. At the door is a clergyman he faintly recognises
from school and Frank Bulmer senior, his hand extended.

Shaking hands the old man looks Toby squarely in the eyes.

"It's so very good to have you back, Toby. So very good.
We know you couldn't get here on time. Your Dad
understood. By the way, I'm the Mayor these days. Case
you're wonderin'. Please come in. We don't want this to be

a sad day. More a day of celebration of a life well-lived and man so loved and .... well, a new beginning."
Friendly arm round his shoulder.
The hall inside is huge and it is full. Was it always so grand? The clergyman pats Toby on the back as they proceed. Frank Bulmer is saying, "Y'know, I think I ate at Whytes just about every day for the last twenty years. Even after the menu got changed. Didn't spoil it for me. Just got better and better."
People are all standing and staring and smiling.
"We have a seat for you at the front."
"This hall, it's a lot bigger than I remember."
Frank looks and nods. "Course, you haven't seen it. When the government slapped the heritage order on the whole town. Y'know, after your Dad became famous. They wouldn't let us touch a thing on the facades of all the buildings, so all we could do was expand everything out the back."
Dad? Famous? What?

Now at the front of the hall, the clergyman takes Toby's arm.
"I'm Peter Prentice. We went to school together."
Oh yes. He has that same needy, please remember me look on his face. They shake hands. It worked, he is remembered.
"Hello Peter, it's good to catch up."
"Your Dad is out the back. We know you'd want a moment to reacquaint." The little man inclined his head toward a door at the side of the stage.
"Please take as long as you like. The town will wait. It will be

a lot to take in. You'll need time to think."

It is sitting on two carpenter's sawing horses. There are some lace-edged coverings on the sawing horses, perhaps in an effort to add a little dignity. From the door it is obviously a very expensive and ornate coffin. The lid is up. Toby Whyte closes his eyes. Alone with his father after twenty years. Finally, tentatively stepping forward, his approach reveals the older version of the man he left all those years ago. When he said the most vile, hurtful things. Words that could never be taken back.

'No, he did not want to eventually take over the running of some six table cafe in some forgotten town.' With his mother dead he was the only child, the chosen one. Too much to bear. He left, got out.

They did begin to talk again after a time. In awkward long-distance phone calls. He had learnt more skills than he realised working with his father in the little kitchen. As his success grew and he became one of the chosen few in Paris his father had seemed pleased. Not once did they broach the subject of his abrupt departure, to make his fortune. Nor a visit, to see each other again.

Eventually, he did introduce the subject of a visit or his father coming to Paris. Both parties were keen. Time was their enemy. Why was his father so busy? Surely the town could handle his absence for a while?

Somebody had done an excellent job on preparing his father. The man looked content, almost happy. It was a fault in the French funeral system that they tried too hard. Funerals he had attended in his new home where the star was on show invariably displayed a tarted-up caricature that was all of sad, comic and abhorrent at once. It ruined farewells for many.

"Something we do right in Australia," he pondered.

"Dad, you're looking okay," he said.

In the silence that followed tears formed while he stood and looked down on the man. He had no disrespect. He loved this man. He thought of his wife and the children back in Montaigne. This was their grandfather. Then he sobbed. Unashamed and also very ashamed. He touched his father's cheek. Surprised somehow that is was quite cold. He stood a moment longer, as if waiting for a signal.

Finally, he reached out and took the solid cream envelope that lay tucked into his father's two clasped hands. Was there a little flour dust adhering to his fingernails?

"There's a letter for you," Peter Prentice had said as he left and closed the door.

The letter was well glued shut.

Dear Toby

I have cancer. The medical people say I have six months at best. What to do? I thought of telling you but what would it

*prove? You're a very busy man these days and it would be
a major inconvenience for you to drop everything and rush
away. I considered flying over and paying you and your family
a surprise visit. But I thought that your wife meeting her father-
in-law and the children meeting their grandfather for a first and
last time would not be very fulfilling for any of us.
So decided to tell you at the last moment. Maybe you'll make it
if you decide to come. I sure hope you do.*

*Okay, now it's confession time. I'm not a religious man but a
good confession I believe will make my going a little easier.
You see I've not been entirely honest with you about how
things were going back here in our town. When you started
getting recognition in France and finally made it to Paris I
followed your career with great interest.
One day serving up my hearty beef casserole to the usual
locals at the cafe I thought, this isn't really that different to a
good French Provincial Cassoulet. So a few days later I dished
up a pork casserole with beans and herbs. The customers
loved it. Next I tried duck dishes, then goose. No rejection, no
"what's this rubbish?" I was onto something. It's then that I
decided I would go all the way. I'd recreate your famous Paris
establishment right here in town.
I copied your menu, recreated a version of your recipes.
Learnt the tricks and subtleties of your work. It took time.
Didn't always get it quite right. You're bloody clever and very
secretive but I obtained a lot of the missing pieces during our*

phone conversations.

Your herbs and spices were sometimes hard to find in this country. Real Saffron for instance. Truffles too. Of course now there are two truffle farmers just outside town.

The turning point was when a small busload of tourists had a mechanical issue and so finished up having dinner at the cafe. They went nuts about it. Two of them were foodie journalists. Within a few weeks, I was overwhelmed. In order to keep this confession short I'll skip the phases of the rebirth. Suffice to say 'Whytes' is substantially larger than you remember it. (Once you get through the doors.) Seating for up to eighty. We became famous. I have staff. A giant kitchen. Everybody in the town made money from the hordes calling for lunch or dinner. Booking essential, weeks in advance. The two big hotels had to be built out of town because of the heritage order. By the way, I have a large portrait of you on the wall complete with your Michelin stars.

Now for the difficult part. I haven't told you any of this stuff because I wasn't sure whether you'd be pleased or horrified and I really didn't want to start another conflict. I mean our phone calls and online communications over recent years have been a real pleasure. Chatting to your wife and the kiddies was lovely. The little videos were so pleasing. Them all running about and playing.

The chefs I have at 'Whytes' are quite good and competent but there's no way any of them could take on the task of running the menu, your menu. It's a little too complex.

Everybody knew I was dying. No secrets in our town as you'd remember. (Most people thought you were a horrible little .... for leaving by the way.)

Anyway, in desperation, with all the town in turmoil about what was going to happen if 'Whytes' closed, I told them not to worry that my dear son Toby was coming back and was going to take over running the establishment. All would be well.

I'm guessing round about now you're sitting next to my coffin holding this letter and you're either red-faced and extremely angry or white-faced and horrified. (Which is why I arranged, even if you did make it to see me before I went, to have this letter with me in the casket.)

So that's it Toby. A horrible thing to do to a 3-star chef but it's my dying wish.

We're pretty famous. I was worried you might hear about us or see some of the publicity on your way. You could possibly get your stars again right here. (He said optimistically.) Maybe a branch of your French operation.

And to close please hear this, Toby.

I love you son with all my heart. I never stopped. Even the day you left. You didn't realise what you were saying. I had forgiven

*you before you reached the airport. I am so very proud of you
and happy for you. Would have liked to have met your wife
and the grandkids but that's the way life is at times. I felt like I
knew them from our talks and the photos and letters.*

*Please, sit and think for a while before you go back out.
Consider the possibilities.*

Your Father (Dad)

Toby Whyte sat for a while. He paced. He muttered. He stood
for some time with his head against the wall. He returned to
the coffin and stared at its occupant as if waiting for the man
inside to smile or wink.

Finally, he sat on a chair with his head in his hands. He sat
there as minutes slid by. Slowly he became aware of the
utter silence surrounding him. Just beyond that door were
a hundred or more people, all, he suspected, collectively
holding their breath. His eyes widened.

"Oh," he said quietly.

He stood and walked back to the coffin. He looked at the
serene countenance of his father, his Dad, then he smiled. It
was a gentle and knowing smile. Somehow, they were both
enjoying the moment.

"Dad, what have you done?" he said at last, "Well, I'm going out now to tell everybody my decision." He patted his father's hands.

Then he turned, took a serious intake of breath and walked to the door to face the crowd.

THE VISITOR

"**E**xcuse me. I used to live here."
In the half-shadow of the hallway, the woman who had
answered the soft knock at her door, stood in her bath-robe.
She was warm and damp from her shower. A cool breeze
flicked about in the street at the end of the garden and
touched her hair.
He sought her eyes through the fly screen door.
"It's something I felt I needed to do. A whim." He paused,
mouth open a little.
"Could I ..... see inside?"

In the silence, the woman tried to process the information

from the man who had interrupted her shower. It took twenty seconds.

Finally, she said, with a half-smile.

"No. I'm sorry, no." She looked into his face. "You may be a very nice man but I can't let you into my home. I don't know you. I don't know anything about you. It's not a situation I want to get into."

Perhaps she expected a protest. A plea to be given a chance. Some reasoning to take place.

"That's alright." He paused. "I'd probably say the same thing. Sorry to bother you." The man looked disappointed.

He half-turned and stopped. Looked back along the wide wooden verandah to the big yard with the equally big plane tree in its centre.

"So green. You expect things to be different. Nothing has changed," he said softly. "It's like I was ten again."

He gave a brief nod and began to make his way down the front steps to the path.

"Oh God," said the woman. "Wait." She pulled her bathrobe tighter around her body.

"I think you might be mistaken. Perhaps you can tell me some things about this house. Convince me you're genuine. How long ago? Tell me something that others wouldn't know. Can you do that?"

The man had stopped on the steps. He did not turn

immediately. Just stood.

He spoke at last with a voice so full of cares and wishes and magical things.

"There are so many stories. I hope you have the time."

When he turned in her direction once more he was smiling. Not at her but at some past, the memories and deeds that he carried like a traveller's portmanteau.

He sat on the little cast iron seat next to the round cast iron table. It had been cleaned up and painted white since he had seen it last.

"Wait here," she had said, pointing along the verandah.

"I'll get some tea and cake and you can give me your story. It will need to be a good story".

She locked the front door and he waited, looking about, noticing things.

When she emerged she carried a tray. He saw her properly for the first time. A lovely old fashioned prettiness. In jeans and slip-on shoes. Her light hair clipped back. A white t-shirt that said, 'Loco' and then 'Motives' on the front.

He jumped up and took the tray.

"I didn't ask'" she said. "Would you have preferred coffee?"

"I love tea. Did you make the cake? Just I haven't seen an orange sponge for years."

They sat and sipped their tea. He asked for a second piece of cake.

"What changed your mind? I mean to give me a chance?"
She smiled over her cup.
"Two things. See that house across the road." She indicated with her head.
The man squinted. The streets were wide and empty.
"Harry lives there. He never misses anything. If you were up to no good, he'd be over here with his shovel as quick as that."
She snapped her fingers.
"He's watching us right now."
"Okay.   .... What's the other reason?"
"I think you're lying and I want to know why."

The man put his cup down. He put his hands between his knees and lowered his head. But the woman spoke first.
"I've lived here all my life. My Dad died before I was born. When I married, my husband moved in here with me. So how could you have lived here?"
The man chuckled.
"This is delicate. I'm older than you I think."
"You said you grew up here. I heard you say ten."
The man sighed.
"It all ended when I was twelve. We moved away. You must have been the next owners."

The woman looked puzzled. "Well, it's possible I suppose. What can you tell me about this place? Come on, convince

me. You better make it good fella."
And so it began.

"The concrete path to the front steps. It curves except for
one flat spot. Dad ran out of timber to form it up so just used
two bricks for the last bit.
The skirting board in the hallway has a bit cut into it near
the second doorway. Termites got into the house and it had
to be repaired.
Harry across the road is the son of Harry. His father used to
be a carpenter and Harry junior wanted to be an electrician.
He was five years-old but he wanted to be an electrician.
This table used to be green. If you scrape off some of the
white you will see the green.
There's a squeaky board just outside my room in the hall.
When I got up to go to have a pee at night the noise woke my
mother. My father was always going to fix it.
My parents used to dance to radio music on the back
verandah. If me and my brother were around they used to
do silly dances to make us laugh. Dad knocked over a lamp
once. It shorted and burnt the panelling near the door.
We were very happy. Mum was a great cook. Biscuits, cakes,
roasts. Fancy stuff as well.
Dad said he worked so hard because it was the only way he
could keep his weight down."

The woman watched her visitor as he spoke. His face was

serene. He wasn't talking to her. He was somewhere else, back in time, walking through his past. A past that had happened someplace and now it had landed here.

She held up her hand to stop the man as he ran barefoot through the wet grass with his brother.
"Please. You're going to make me cry." She paused and then, looked the man in the eye. "Here's the only answer I can give. Will you come back tomorrow? I'm not going to let you in my house today. My husband is at work and my boys are at school."
The man stared back.
"Yes," he said, "I can do that."

As they parted the woman called, "Where did you go? When you moved."
"We went toward the sun. My Mum had died. Dad said he just wanted somewhere warm."
As the man walked down the path to the gate the woman called.
"I don't know your name."
He turned.
"My name is Carl. What's yours?"
"Junee. My name is Junee."

Harry sat at the kitchen table. He looked from Junee to her

husband Luke. The boys poked at their food, more interested in the story of the strange visitor than their moussaka.

"You think he's got the wrong house. But he knows a lot. Maybe he just visited the place. You know had really strong memories of some good times here when he was young. Perhaps he knew the previous owners. My Dad used to tell me that the bloke here just up and left, overnight, while his wife was in the hospital having their next kid. That is what you call a lousy thing to do."

"Why did he leave?" asked Ben.

His mother looked at the eight-year-old.

"You just get on with your eating young man."

Luke leaned back in his chair his arms behind his head. He was a handsome man. Tanned and strong from his arborist work.

"Funny isn't it. Your Mum just won't talk about your Dad. Once he died of his heart attack it's as though he ceased to exist. Was she heartbroken, angry, shocked? Never been able to tell."

"Well," said Junee, "By the time I was old enough to ask questions, he was a distant memory. Just one photo."

Luke looked at Harry.

"What happened to the woman and her baby?"

Harry screwed up his face.

"I don't know. I was only a little guy when it happened. I

never really understood the ins and outs of it all. Dad and Mum were pretty protective of Junee's Mum though. I mean after her father died."

Harry stopped and lifted his finger.

"Where's your deeds to this house? If they're the old type of deeds they'll have the names of the previous owner listed on the document."

Luke looked at his wife.

"We don't own the place. Junee's Mum still owns it. She's got it set up to leave to us in her Will. Said it didn't seem much point transferring the title when we were going to get it anyway."

"Well we could ask?" Junee held up her arms. "Mum hasn't seen the boys for a couple of weeks. It's only up the road."

"Benny, Mark!" Junee's Mum held out her arms for a hug. The boys obliged.

"The doorman gave us the third degree again," said Luke.

"Well, we're only old people in this place dear. He has to be protective." The old lady smiled and patted her lounge chair for them all to be seated.

"So, what has brought you all here and even Harry, at this time of night. I hope it's something nice."

Junee looked at her mother. "It's a little bit of a mystery

Mum. Can we see the deeds to the house?"

Junee met Carl at the front gate. Her face had changed. He couldn't tell if it was anger or something deeper.

"Don't go any further mister. I want to talk to you."

This was his second visit for the day. When he'd arrived at 10am he was told to go away and come back at 4pm. Now standing in the warmth of a long summer with butterflies and buzzing creatures moving about in the afternoon air he waited for the woman to continue.

"How old are you?"

"I'm 45 since you ask."

"And I'm 33." Junee glared at the man in front of her. "How did your mother die?"

"She died in childbirth."

"And so you just packed up and left?"

"Well we didn't pack up. Dad came home from the hospital. He just put us in the car and we left. We drove pretty much non-stop for two days until we came to this little town and Dad said, 'This will do.' He told us about a year later that he couldn't go back in the house. Not alone. I think I understood. My mother was the light of his life. They were two people who became one. When she died it was as if he had been torn in half. He died ten years later. I don't know if there's a medical condition for a broken heart but I'm pretty sure that's what killed him."

"Did you stay in the town?"

"We did. We wanted to be near Dad. My younger brother
Steve was killed last year. A huge truck hit his car just
outside town. He was the only relative I had in the world, so
I said to my wife and our two daughters that I wanted to go
on a little road trip. You know, just to have a look at my past.
Cathartic exercise if you like. And here I am. Nothing sinister.
Just looking over the old town."

Junee continued to stare.

"This is odd. I found all this stuff in one of our spare rooms
when I was about seven. Boys' toys and clothes. Mum got
angry and said they belonged to the previous tenants. I
wasn't allowed to touch them again. They could have been
yours."

The two figures stood idly at the gate. The sun was warm.
Birds flitted about in the trees over their heads.

"What's your surname?"

"LeCroix," the man said. "I'm Carl LeCroix. Why do you ask?"

"Just that there's something not right about you or about
that time. You left. Mum and I moved in. Odd."

"You keep saying odd. Seems fairly straight forward to me."

"So how did your Dad sell the house?"

"I'd imagine he contacted an agent who contacted another
agent and it was done through some network."

Junee looked around at the garden. She said distantly. "We asked my mother to show us the deeds of this house last night. She said she didn't have them. That they were in safe-keeping with her Will." Junee waved her hands about. "This is …. this is all strange. Family in the house, their mother dies and they leave. Next family in the house. Briefly I think. The husband abandons wife while she's in hospital having their first child. Then Mum moves in with baby me."

The two people stood awkwardly at the gate.

"Why are we talking here?

"Because we invited my mother over. She's sitting in our loungeroom. She doesn't know about you. I thought it might be interesting for her to meet the man who owned those clothes you left behind."

"It would be interesting. Lots of notes to compare."

Junee took Carl's arm.

"I've got one final question. This is the clincher Carl leCroix. If you were a ten year old and you lived here, you climbed trees right?"

"Sure did."

"Then you'd know that there's a secret hole way up in one of the branches in that tree."

She pointed to the backyard plane tree.

"My boys discovered it a couple of years back. They found something in the hole. Can you tell me what they found and translate?"

In the silence the late summer cicadas started up again.

The man stood with his head down, staring at the path,
his hand to his mouth. He remained transfixed for nearly a
minute then lifted his head in triumph.

"Two pieces of aluminium, shaped like shields. One is blue
with a yellow diagonal stripe. The other is red with a yellow
diagonal stripe. On the back of each would be the initials
HDC. I was Dogman and Steve was Catman. In French that's
'homme de chien' and 'homme de chat.'"

Junee had tears in her eyes.
"Wait till I tell the boys I know what HDC means."

A car slid to a halt next to the gate. As they watched, Harry
climbed out of the driver's seat and went to the other side.
He opened the passenger side door to reveal an elderly lady
who did not smile and looked in some distress.
"I have somebody I'd like you to meet." he said. "Prepare to
have your lives altered a little. Maybe we should sit in the
car while we talk."

Half an hour later Carl and Junee walked back along the
path to the house. They held hands.
Both were pale.
Carl could hardly speak. "I'm shaking. This is not a simple
visit anymore."
As they entered the hallway a voice called out from the

loungeroom.

"Is that you Junee? Where have you been dear?"

Junee gripped the man's hand.

"Come on Carl, I'm here with you. Things are different now."

They entered the room and stood. Luke and the boys looked

on. Facing her mother Junee said, "Mum, there's somebody

I'd like you to meet."

Carl looked at the lady in the large armchair. His heart raced.

He thought he saw a sudden change in her expression.

"Hullo Mum," he said, "It's me, Carl."

The woman let out a small scream. A mixture of thirty six

years of misery, heartache sorrow, love and confusion.

As the old lady in the car had talked she had cried. She told

Junee, Carl and Harry of the night when she was young and

was the matron on duty in their small maternity hospital.

Two women suddenly went into labour late at night. Just she

and Dr Penman had struggled alone to deliver the babies.

It was terrible. There were complications. They did their

best. One of the women and her baby died. The other gave

birth and settled. Just then a man appeared at the front desk

to inquire about his wife. The nurse thought she knew the

man. What could she do? There was no alternative. She told

him the awful truth. That his wife and child had died.

The man was overwhelmed. He left in a terrible state. Just

walked out the door into the night.

Next morning as she completed her notes for the records she realised she had given the tragic news to the wrong man. When she went to speak to the fellow at his home, to put things right, she was told that he and his boys had gone. Nobody knew where. Horrified at what she had done she decided to keep her secret and say nothing.

She heard later that the wife who had been abandoned because of her mistake, now lived in the house alone with her young girl. They used the mother's maiden name and the wife never mentioned the missing husband or her two boys. And that is the way it stayed until today when Harry came to her house and began asking questions, about the night Junee was born.

It was time to unburden herself and accept the terrible wrong. She could not go to her grave without confessing.

"When are they coming?"

Carl looked up at his wife then at his children.

"Next week."

The story had taken a while to tell. They sat in his garden. A lush green garden with a big tree, so much like that other garden of his youth. It was the first time he had noticed the similarity.

"I'm going to the cemetery this afternoon. I want to sit and tell my father and my brother. Tell them what might have been."

The man looked again at his family. They sat wide-eyed, seeking some ways to find a positive in the news and the prospect of a new family branch.

Carl held his hands out in a gesture of frustration.

"I don't know why life does what it does to us all. It unfolds and you live with the consequences."

Cicadas made a lazy attempt at starting up their summer throb but faded. A magpie gave a burbling call announcing its territory. Far off a goods train rolled through their local crossing. The sequence of sound ended and silence returned.

Carl's wife leaned forward and patted her husband's knee. "Are you glad you went?" she whispered .... "You said it would be a 'cathartic exercise'."

Carl looked away across the garden, across places and events, time and circumstances. He took a breath and then nodded.

"Yeah," he said, "I'm glad I went. For old times sake. For a moment I was back there. Barefoot and ten. It was all okay then."

ON THE RIDGE

On the fourth day at 10am.

A rock overhang appears above. It juts out of the steep side
of the slope like an eagle's beak. Even a hooked drop of stone
could be seen at its end. Its outer point reached well beyond
the thick foliage creating a possible viewing platform.

He liked the pace. There is no pressure to achieve, to be
anywhere. Just the now. Yes, he wanted to reach the rock,
to stand on its granite bulk and consider all that he had
accomplished and for that matter gain some perspective on
his progress but when and how he arrived was not of great
importance. It was the freedom to choose, the flippancy with
which he could take or leave time. And it was only the fourth

day.

He stood, because he could, for some minutes, just silent,
enjoying the minor movements and inventions of the earth
about him. Reaching out refusing to take a step he slid his
fingers onto the cool bark of a mid-size Tallow Wood.
It soared over him through the canopy on a quest for the sky.
He allowed himself several small sips from his water bottle
while examining a way to the rock overhang. It would not be
easy, dangerous perhaps but rewarding.

It was not, easy. He had slipped at one stage. A potential fatal
drop off the side of this unforgiving lump onto more rocks
and foliage. His body would have crashed away down the
slope to finish God knows where?
His fingers held. Anger and gritted teeth bore him upwards.
In retrospect, he should have climbed with just a rope
running back to his pack. He could then have hauled it
up afterward. Backpacks change your balance. They drag
you away and tilt you, like some fiendish child on your
shoulders.
Sitting, breathing hard, a little frightened, he forced himself
to lay back and let the flat, solid top of the overhang reassure
him with its mass and security.
The view was pleasing and immense. A whole giant valley of
nothing but wild, green rainforest. The extensive emptiness
found in the north, in the Tropic of Capricorn.
It was this frisson of fear that had brought him here and

now captured his thoughts. He'd picked a point on a map and said to himself, "That is where I'll go." It seemed remote enough to ensure some solitary time. Being sufficiently alone was all he craved. If he did not ever return nor was ever seen again, it would not matter. Though he did ponder a little on the aftermath of his possible demise.

How long before anybody notices? Would there be any inquiry as to what might have become of him? Would anybody care or would the world simply continue and some bureaucracy in some blank building, take care of the paperwork.

In the end, he had included a small laminated card in a pocket of his backpack that simply gave his name. At least somebody finding his remains would have a name.

Seated on the great flat rock, his feet out, leaning on his elbows he could turn his head and see the top of the ridge. It formed the northern side of the valley.

On climbs before he had been led astray by summits that kept moving away as you ascended. This ridge-top may be the same, though it appeared not to have any deceptive higher layers beyond the part he could see. Whatever it presented, he planned to be there at nightfall, hopefully much sooner.

Perhaps as nature's way of an apology, the final climb to the rim above was relatively easy. A spongy water-course led down to the back of the rock overhang. He imagined water cascading off the rock from all sides in heavy rain. Only the last thirty metres were a struggle as a tangle of ferns and bushes hung off the rim like a web. They were filled with small birds. A sort of avian hotel.

In a final thrashing push, he thrust his face and shoulders through into the light and reached up to a line of hard rock that gave a decent grip. He hauled himself and then his pack up and onto the top of the bushes then shoved his pack above him and over the rock line. At the last moment as he let go of his pack he considered that the other side of the rock may be deceptive and fall away but when he dragged his nose over the rock he could see quite a large open area with his pack lying there on its back.

He sat for some minutes on the edge of the rock admiring the massive valley he had traversed.

It was mid-afternoon. His objective achieved he felt relief. Almost like coming home.

It took an hour to become comfortable. The place he had found on the top of the ridge seemed close to perfect. It was flat and level except for a deep crease to one side that must be a watercourse from elsewhere when rain swept over the area. He cleared away debris and leaf litter. A dent in the surrounding bushes provided a protected set-back for his tent. He could lay in the tent's mouth and look out over the valley. To the left front of the tent, he scraped out a hollow in the soft soil to provide a fire pit. He dragged several large bush branches down close to the ground, covered them in plastic bags and tied them off. Already in the heat, he could see a pool of condensate forming in the base of the bags to provide a water supply.

Closer to the edge of the ridge a series of rocks stacked upon the rim suggested an improvement waiting to be made. By wrenching a large central rock from the pile, an almost perfect armchair emerged with the dislodged rock forming a foot-stool. The man stood back and gave a small laugh.

He wiped his mouth. Nobody would see this tiny world he had created.

On a plastic sheet in front of the tent, he lay out his supplies and equipment. It was a calculated assortment. He had suffered the crushing weight of his pack for days so that he could have this degree of enjoyment.

All the food was dry. Water being crucial to meal preparation. Rice, peas, corn, barley, apricot, sultanas, noodles, salt, pepper, sugar, Malay curry powder, milk powder, gravy mix, onion, stock cubes, beef strips, pasta, potato mix, tea, instant coffee and more, all laid out in labelled clip-lok plastic bags.

Fire flint in case his matches became wet or ran out.

To prepare what he hoped would be a varied and enjoyable menu he unfolded a set of three aluminium pans and small pressure stove.

Since the commencement of the walk he had eaten only
energy bars. Tonight he intended to have a fine meal.
A reward to himself for his efforts. Briefly, again, he realised
that he was the only person who knew or cared where he
was, what he was doing or the eloquence of his planned
evening repast. He felt resigned to the way it was. Dropping
from existence was somewhat easy if your connections to
existence were tenuous at best.
From the start, he knew this journey might be that of one
direction. He was content with the concept.

Now he sat for a while in his armchair holding the large
plastic container of water that he had carried from the valley
floor. Down there, streams and watercourses were abundant.
Fresh, clean, pure of taste. On these heights, he was not sure
of a supply. The plastic sweat bags on the bushes seemed to
be working but not in great quantity.
"To hell with it," he said, "I'm thirsty."
He drank greedily. Even tipped a little in his hand and wiped
his face. He let the faint breeze cool his skin. He looked at
the water container once more. Enough for his meal. Enough
for tomorrow.

With a fire crackling in the pit the man lay back and sipped
a brew of coffee. His meal sat in his belly. He was not
happy. It was a feeling he found impossible to create. The
best he could summon up was satisfaction. A feeling of

accomplishment. He was here where he planned to be. Although the night was warm he leaned forward and let the flames heat his face. It felt good. He lifted his head, stared at the mass of stars overhead and finally said, "Now what, my friend. Where does this end?"

For the moment he waited. There was no answer.

At 9pm he slid into his sleeping bag, placed his large hunting knife beside his head, zipped his tent closed and lay down. Within a minute he slept.

At 10.15pm he was awoken by a noise close to his face. Sniffing, snuffling on the other side of the tent's cloth. The creature was making its way along the side of the tent. It could smell all the food the man had taken into his tent for safekeeping. Carefully, slowly, removing his arm from the sleeping bag, he waited until the creature's shadow came level with his shoulder. He then punched the side of the tent and the firm, furry object outside. There was an urgent scrabbling sound. It picked itself up from the blow and scuttled away in a startled hurry through the ground cover. The man then slept without disturbance until the tent became quite bright in the morning light.

The first day on the ridge the man did very little. He walked a few hundred metres along the ridge each side of his campsite. The ridge was quite level though heavily tangled with tropical undergrowth. To the left, about 50 metres, there appeared to be a trodden track, though it was not very distinct. There would not be any large animals to create such a path, so in the end it was determined to be an anomaly and nothing more.

The walks did convince the visitor that he had found by chance the most desirable site in the area for his camp.

He idled the late afternoon watching birdlife from his rock armchair. There was a distinct difference in the urgency of life in his new location. Birds on the coast appeared frantic, constantly observing, watching, flicking about in a nervous survival dance. Here they were of a more languorous mood. Their pace was easy. They took time to sit and observe, to preen and only occasionally give a call, as almost a duty rather than any territorial necessity.

He could name a few. Riflebird, Bridled Honeyeater, Thornbill, Parrot Finch. He even had a visit from a green and red Eclectus Parrot.

The man slept late. He woke with a level of peace within that he had not felt for some time. It took some seconds when he opened his eyes to adjust his mind to where he was and his situation.

The plastic bags on the surrounding bushes were working adequately. He collected enough condensated water for his needs, for breakfast, some coffee maybe even a wash.

He stood on the edge of the ridge this morning, naked and wet allowing the soft breeze moving up from the valley to cool his skin. With his eyes closed, his arms outstretched it would have been so easy to fly away.

He spent more time fixing up his site. He cleared the bushes
back from his tent, then dug a drainage channel around the
area to take away any heavy rain.

He found various flat rocks and laid out a raised area next
to his armchair. At waist-height it allowed him to move his
cooking materials onto a workable platform.

Surveying the work he felt more 'at home' than he had for
some years.

With his piece of climbing rope tied between two trees he
had a washing line if not the water to carry out the task.

Lunch consisted of crackers with processed cheese and tea
made with powdered milk. It seemed inadequate. He took
the bag and emptied his food supply out onto his new work
platform then paired up various items creating meals in
his mind. With some sacrifice, he could stay for two weeks.
Maybe a little more. He stood and considered his situation
tapping his nose with his finger. While experienced in hiking
and survival he had never forced himself to 'live off the
land'. Perhaps it was time to look about. Options may exist.
Plunging straight into the bushes behind his tent he aimed
for a giant tree that could be seen further in on the ridge.
With a compass bearing to its location, he had a way in and
out. The tree disappeared as he worked his way under the
canopy of green growth tied together with vines and ferns.
He carried a large hunting knife on his belt and a sharpened

pole in his hand. He made his way up a slight rise and the undergrowth thinned. Suddenly the tree, a Kauri, appeared in front with a relatively open area around its base. The tree itself was on a small raised island. From its base, the man could make out an unusual peaked rock formation. It stood well above the rainforest in from the edge of the ridge about 500 metres away. He made a note to explore that area in the following days. Closer by was a large Strangler Fig.
Its base roots had several little pockets containing water which tasted brackish. Some fruit lay about the ground. The man bit into some. They were full of tiny seeds. The taste was bearable. He collected some. Maybe boiled with the addition of some sugar. There were other berries but they tasted bitter or alkaline and downright dangerous. Still, on return to his camp, the man had some hope that he might find items to supplement his rations. He had seen nothing on which he could have used his sharpened pole.

Once again he slept well. Laying just under his sleeping bag rather than in it due to the heat. No nocturnal disturbances from the local fauna. When morning came he slept on till the tent was quite light and bright.
What finally woke him or seeped into his subconscious was a crackling sound. Rainforest is full of sound. It becomes the background to every part of existence within its confines. But this sound was foreign. Crackling was not a normal sound. As he reached a conscious state, his mind recognised

the sound. It was fire. Could there be a forest fire beginning? Now he panicked. Scrambling to roll into an upright position he lunged at the tent front and tugged the zips open, thrusting his head out expecting perhaps a wall of flame.

His fire was burning gently in his fire hole. He could not comprehend its ability to self-combust. Then he saw a man sitting in his armchair, looking his way.

The man spoke.

"Good morning. Hope I didn't startle you. Always nice to have a fire going in the morning I think. That way you can heat up some water and then you can say, make coffee."

He paused, looking, smiling at the head poking from the tent flap.

"Please tell me you've got some coffee."

They sat quietly, sipping hot black coffee. The visitor had graciously given up the armchair and was seated cross-legged on the ground near the fire.

He spoke finally in his amiable way.

"So, as I said, you could have just told me you don't have coffee. I may have believed you. Precious stuff up here."

He downed the last of his cup.

"Oh hell, that was good."

The visitor stood and walked to the cliff edge.

"At risk of repeating myself. What are the chances? There can't be another body within 50 kilometres in any direction.

Here we are side by side. Wonder if there's some odd reason. You don't have a secret message for me or anything do you?" He turned to his host in the armchair.

The man smiled.

"No, sorry. I just paddled up the river until I caught a glimpse of the escarpment then hid the canoe and headed on in. All I wanted to do was get up on top of some part of it."

"That's it. Simple answer."

"What?"

"First time you get a brief clear view of the escarpment. It's on the bend, bit of a pool, big tree down, pushed the foliage over, so you get a view. Bet you parked your canoe next to mine without knowing. Isn't life strange."

The visitor had an agitated manner, as if he had many thoughts all moving about in his head. He walked back and forth along the cliff edge then returned to the fire holding out his hands in mock need of the heat. He had a large frame. As if his arms and legs were a size too big. He wore shorts and a slightly frayed shirt. On his feet were some heavy-duty leather sandals. His hair was in a ponytail, held with some string. If he had really been here for five months, as he said, he was surprisingly clean and tidy.

The visitor spoke again.

"Look, I wasn't sure whether to pay you a visit or not but yesterday when I saw you looking over my way, looking at my rock castle I thought, he's gonna find his way here sooner or later, better go and say hullo. Which brings up this next bit. I'd like to invite you to dinner tonight. It will be a stew. After that, we'll decide whether we want to keep saying hullo or we ignore each other. I came up here to get away from people because people just drive me crazy. I've been back down once and I confirmed that they still drove me crazy. Picked up some more bits and pieces and headed back. Could be you're the same and I don't want to ruin that for you so see you tonight."

He turned to go before spinning back around.

"Don't s'pose it'll hurt to know each other's names."

He held out his hand. "I'm Stuart."

The man in the armchair stood and took the hand.

"I'm Jason."

Heading off into the scrub Stuart called back over his shoulder.

"Take that half a track you were looking at, it'll see you to my front door. Thanks again for the coffee."

Late afternoon Jason followed the track. It was faint but it did lead ever closer to the large 'castle' like rock he had seen the previous day. It, in fact, grew larger as he approached, much larger.

All-day he had considered the strange event of the morning. It still unnerved him slightly. Was he missing anything? His quest for solitude lasted only a few days and here he was going out to dinner. The notion of being alone and deciding his fate given over to an uneasiness about a new circumstance.

He thought he could smell something pleasant as he drew nearer. With the suddenness of stepping through a thin waterfall he was out of the heavy green underbrush and into a clearing.

On the other side, sitting in what was a substantial open cavern was Stuart. He was sitting at a table. There were four chairs. A second larger table appeared to be a workbench.

"What does a bloke do with a lot of spare time, a machete, a knife and an axe?" Stuart called. "He builds furniture."

Seated at Stuart's table with a plastic cup of water and some lumpy biscuits Jason continued to look about marvelling at the homeliness of his host's abode.

"You said you only went back once. This amount of equipment would take more than one trip."

"It did," Stuart said. "I came up here when I just didn't want to be near people anymore. Found this place and set up camp. Stayed weeks till I was running out of everything. When it came time to leave I realised how much I liked it here. So I made a list. Crept back, saw nobody. Bought everything on my list. Packed the canoe till it was nearly sinking and headed back up the river. Took me four trips to get all the gear from the canoe to this place but it was worth it."

Stuart stood and beckoned his guest.

"Come and look at this."

At the side of the rocks, half enclosed by the stone wall, heavily fenced and covered in netting was a vegetable garden.

"I bought seed packets back with me. Potatoes, corn, pumpkin. Easy to grow and filling. Tomatoes are hard. Too many bugs like them. Now come here."

He led his visitor back into the cavern, continuing to the rear. Where the wall seemed to end he stepped round into a dark area that sloped downward. There was a sound. Water dripping. As his eyes became accustomed to the light Jason could make out a large pool of crystal clear water in the stone base.

"Filters through the area, drips down through the rock and finishes up here. Never stops. Even organised some mushrooms that are edible."

The biscuits were cornmeal. Now they sat and ate a hearty, stew.

"What's the meat?"

"Snake," said Stuart. "Not what you expected eh. Tastes good and eliminates danger. Win, win for me."

The two men ate in silence for a minute then Stuart spoke.

"Do you have a God?"

Jason stopped, his spoon halfway to his mouth.

"No. Never been able to reconcile the creation of super-beings to cover the unknowns. Hope I didn't offend."

Stuart gave a little laugh.

"That's a damned relief. I had this heart-skipping moment where I thought you might be on some religious pilgrimage. Gonna stop now. Your reasons for moving into nowhere are strictly yours. Just say, I'd had enough of the Dreamtime, Jesus, God thing when I headed out of town."

"You're aboriginal? I wouldn't have picked it."

"About one-tenth," said Stuart. "Just enough to be annoying. Too many relatives, too many muddled ideas. I talk to myself up here. So far the advice has been fine."

The two men conversed until 8pm when the light was beginning to fade. Sparring verbally, neither giving much away.

Finally, Jason said, "I'm going to head back now, while I can find my way. Thanks for the meal. It was a good deal for one cup of coffee."

Stuart shook his hand.

"I saw you had one of those collapsible buckets. If you need water, come along anytime. I may not be here. You'll be right."

Jason did return a few days later. The weather steaming up and his evaporation bags were not supplying sufficient water. The camp was deserted. A little hot and exposed in the sun's midday reign. He walked around and admired Stuart's handiwork and initiative. Many items of comfort hewn from the native timber. The garden was bountiful but he could not take any of the produce. Perhaps because he felt he was being watched. He had several drinks using his cupped hands then filled his bucket and walked slowly back to the ridge.

At nights now he sat with his legs hanging over the edge of the rock cliff thinking of the way things were and how they had evolved for him to where there was no going back.

One late morning he thought he heard a voice or call from down in the valley but it could have been Trumpet Manucode or similar bird. It reminded him of life beyond his eyrie.

Food was now low. He appreciated that he had been left alone by his near neighbour. The man must have sensed it was the situation he preferred and he had reciprocated.

It was time for a decision. He walked for a great distance around the ridgeline admiring the beautiful green mass of the valley below. It looked soft and welcoming. From any angle, the eagle's beak rock platform below his campsite stood out as a beacon for his thoughts.

That evening while twilight still lit the path he made another trip to Stuart's camp. It was to be his last. Once again the place was deserted. It was quiet. A complete stillness. Signs of activity near and around the man's work table but not the man himself.

Jason took some water from the pool and then went to the vegetable garden. There were some sweet potatoes sitting on the ground freshly harvested under the net. He took one, feeling all the while that he was supposed to do so and that Stuart knew.

He boiled the plant up and ate it for a final meal along with some black tea.

Once the sun was up the next morning Jason packed and cleaned up his campsite. He did his best to hide the fact that any person had ever been to the place. In a forgotten corner pocket of his pack he found a sealed plastic bag of scroggin. Prepared before he left some time back it was the only food that remained.

By 10am he sat on the edge of the cliff with his completed, repacked backpack beside him. He looked down across the valley closed his eyes and let out a shuddering sigh. It was time to go.

With an easier descent than the ascent, he reached the back of the flat eagle's beak rock in under fifteen minutes.

He pulled torn pieces of vine from his pack and then dropped it down onto the rock.

For some time thereafter he just stood, looking steadily out along the rock's smooth expanse to the end and the nothingness beyond.

Eventually, as if switched back to life again, he stirred into action and made his way along the whole structure to its narrow point, hanging out over the valley floor below. A wind that did not exist at its base pushed roughly across the point of the rock. There he stood looking not down but straight out to some unknown distant point.

Then he stepped off.

The drop took long enough to be aware of falling. The valley floor, at first an indistinguishable green mass, now became distinct large trees and foliage as his body hurtled towards them. At the moment of impact, he would be smashed and battered and his life destroyed. He would vanish down to the base of some tree to be swallowed in a mass of green understorey and cease to be of any interest to anybody. Unknown, unmissed, forgotten.

In his mind, Jason saw all of this taking place in a rapid, gasping picture show of what might have been, as he swayed on the edge. However, with his eyes wild he stepped back and turned away from the final step he could have taken.

Was he a coward or was there something left?

He returned to his backpack and looked for a line of descent down off the rock.

Above, the man called Stuart nodded to himself at the sight and turned away from the ridgeline disappearing into the bushes.

THE GREEK HARBOUR

Nobody saw him arrive. Though Kristo said he knew
the circumstances by which he came. When pressed the
fisherman admitted his hypothesis was pure speculation.
The young man presented by way of several inquiries at
the side door of the tavern, asking for a room. Spiro was
delighted at the thought of a paying guest in his empty
upstairs rooms. He asked, somewhat despairingly how many
days the man would be his guest?
"Indefinitely," was the answer.
Now Spiro was doubly excited.

The first evening the guest came down to the open tavern

area with its white, lean-on-level outdoor walls, tired grapes growing on tired trellises and sprinkling of half-working lights. It was a place for fishermen and old men to sit and complain about all manner of things that plagued their lives and the world.

The stranger seated himself silently in a corner table against the wall near the sloping side street. He nodded at the men who looked in his direction. He had a leather case in his hand. The observers noted that when opened it was seen to be a writing pad complete with several pencils. The case looked well used. The leather ties that hung from the spine had been fastened and unfastened many times.

Spiro was keen to have his paying guest feel comfortable amongst his regular, somewhat difficult collection of patrons.

"For you. Is welcome plate. No charge, this night," he said, placing a plate of goat cheese, with wedges of lemon, bread chunks and olives, even a pot of fish row taramasalata in front of the man. With a flourish he placed his thumb over the top of a bottle of olive oil and dripped some on the bread. Finally, he added an earthenware jug and a glass.

"Is good local wine. Red colour." Spiro smiled a smile that introduced his exceptional collection of gold teeth.

"I tell everybody you name it is Rufus. That okay?"

The man looked up.

"Yes, of course, thank you."

Spiro half-turned to all those watching as if to say, he says it's okay that you know his name.

The young man nodded in the crowd's direction and they all smiled back and nodded. He was a handsome man they thought. Tanned and with blue eyes. Some had daughters who may be suitable, if this stranger turned out to have some talent or possessed land or money somewhere.

The customers were all aware of the stranger's presence but as the night became darker and the drinks took hold of their minds and mouths the stranger faded into the background in his corner, only to receive an occasional glance when the conversation and gossip briefly lulled. Such glances noted that he sat quietly making notes with his pencil on his paper pad.

Later still a glance revealed that the young man was no longer there, having retired early to his upstairs bed. It was pointed out that he had finished all of Spiro's jug of wine and eaten only the cheese and bread plate so he was at least of sufficient fortitude to still walk after a hearty amount of the massively overproof brew. He would sleep well. And he did.

It was one day short of the first week when Rufus appeared at the door of Spiro's kitchen about midmorning. The cafe owner was unpacking food from the markets. Also fish and other seafood from his friends at the wharf.

"Good morning Mr Rufus. You are well? What is for you to do today?"

The young man took some of the boxes from the back seat of Spiro's tiny Renault. He handed them into Spiro through the doorway from bright sunlight into darkness.

"Ah thank you Rufus. In truth I don't normally do this stuff. The buying and the fetching. My cook, he quit. Says he make more money on the mainland. Want to be big-time cook. Now I got no cook. You cook by any chance?"

Rufus looked down at his sandals. He was wearing the same clothes in which he had arrived. A white muslin shirt and khaki shorts.

"No Spiro sorry. My cooking talents are pretty limited." He rubbed his face and stubbled chin as if in torment then spread his hands toward his host.

"I hate to add more bad news to your day Spiro but well, the truth is, I haven't been entirely honest with you."

Spiro stopped and looked the man over.

"What? You a spy, a criminal, a wife cheater. You not Rufus? You somebody else? It's okay nobody worry too much."

"No Spiro, I'm broke."

Spiro stopped stacking the tomatoes and anchovies.

He stood motionless for some seconds.

"Oh shit Rufus, your rent due tomorrow and the food bill. How much you got?"

"Nothing, as it happens."

Spiro Laskaris was not a man given to rage. He was a thinker. It took some minutes after his only guest's revelation as to his financial status to conjure up a solution that would be of benefit to all but most especially to Spiro. It involved a small amount of mental arithmetic, a large amount of cunning and an offer that on the face of it could not be refused.

By the young man's admission of his indebtedness, Spiro now owned the man. He may as well have had his soul in a hidden casket. The man would have to do whatever was required of him to clear his debt. He could have perhaps simply run away. But where do you run on an island?

The sums in Spiro's head involved the wage that his recently departed cook had earned against the loss of the tiny amount of room rental and food required by young Mr Rufus. The solution was simple. In exchange for his room and his food Rufus would henceforth work on the tables of the cafe, clean, wash up and shop. Spiro would take over the cooking duties. He knew his customers. Townsfolk and fishermen. They liked to sit and gossip, complain and play checkers. Stare at the ocean and harbour and remember past deeds. Occasionally a game of petanque might break out in the side street.

They would not especially miss him wandering about through their tables. They all liked Rufus. He was a novelty. They had quietly adopted him and if they could read English they would have created a diversion by now and scanned the writings in his journal.

Spiro could still make appearances to say hullo. He would be some considerable distance in front when it came to money, with no expensive cook to maintain. He felt happy at the cleverness of his problem solving.

Rufus looked at Spiro.

"I could do that," he said, "it seems most fair. But I don't speak Greek."

Spiro put his large hand on the shoulder of Rufus.

"Hah, is okay most of my customers they not too good understand Greek either. No smart peoples here, just simple. You'll work it out with them. Be fun. Lots of laugh. And that way you learn the Greek soon yourself."

It was hilarious. The customers turned the whole new arrangement into a game ordering ridiculous items and gallons of wine. Rufus ran back and forth while Spiro cooked, asking him to interpret the orders. Spiro laughed, at first. For a while, he joined in the silliness at the expense of his new waiter. However, the game seemed to have no end and the orders soon ceased to be funny and became tiresome. Besides, while the fishermen and townsfolk were requesting sheep's tails and octopus hearts and so on, they were not ordering real food. The type of fare that Spiro could cook and for which they would pay.

He sighed when Rufus arrived with the latest notes. Untying his apron strings and flopping the garment aside he took Rufus by the arm.

"Come with me," he said.

Arm in arm they confronted the happy patrons. Slowly, as
they stood, the laughter and merriment subsided. There
were mutterings and some heads bowed. Spiro waited until
a complete silence enveloped the crowd, then he spoke. His
large dark eyebrows made his eyes particularly serious.
For those who knew the Greek language he said, "My friends,
I feel our amusement at the new waiter's expense has run
its course. While it was funny at the beginning it has now
become foolish and very immature so I ask you to stop.
Rufus is a nice fellow and we should give him a chance.
He has expressed a deep affection for the Greek culture and
Greek people. He wishes most sincerely to learn the Greek
language and become accepted as one of us. Please help him
in his noble quest. And while you are offering your help and
understanding try to find out more about him. My curiosity
is at a high level. Who is this stranger, where is he from
and how and why did he suddenly appear on our tiny little
forgotten Greek island? It is a mystery I wish to solve. You
will be doing both yourselves and me a great service in this
quest. Thank you for your help. Please now pat his back and
tell him he is a fine fellow. Order food."
He paused.
"And no more of the stupid stuff."

Spiro turned and disappeared back into his premises leaving
Rufus staring at the customers. They stared back. Rufus had
not understood any of the words in Spiro's speech except

for the occasional mention of his name but he could read an audience and their faces indicated that all was well. He would never know the lies concerning his love of all things Greek, nor the secret pact that had just formed to extract his life story but these trivialities aside he felt a new beginning had been established.

The crowd suddenly rose as one and surrounded him, laughing and patting his back. Many kissed him on both cheeks including some of the more motherly women.

A young girl with wild hair, dark brown eyes and a knowing smile grabbed his face and briefly took hold of his soul as she kissed him voraciously. His eyes closed Rufus briefly dreamed of her joining him in his room and making the night complete. Then he opened his eyes noted that she had returned to her large, handsome boyfriend and the encounter had been staged.

The night went well after this moment. Food orders were many and varied and carefully spelled out. People helped with their names and thus began the slow process of acquainting the man with their language. After all, they could not strip him of his secrets if they could not communicate with the source.

The more committed met with Spiro after closing time. They shared some awful wine that Spiro could not sell.

"It is hard. He's a slow learner. The few words he has learnt, the yes and the no and food names, they tell us nothing.

It will take years at this rate. Now he does the waiting instead of the writing so we can't even look at his notebook." Another man, a farmer with goats added, "The notes they will be in the English, so we can't read the words anyway. You speak a little English Spiro. Can you read the language?"

"I can make a bit of the conversation, that's all. Can't read any of it."

Spiro took a long mouthful of his wine and winced.

"You know……. what we need is an educated speaker and reader of the English and the greek."

They paused, looking from one to the other.

"There is only Dr Anastas," they replied. "He is an honorable man, he would never do such a thing. He is the only one."

Again they paused looking from one to another for inspiration. It came from Spiro. He raised his forefinger. They all looked at the extended digit. Spiro also had his eyebrows raised and his head tilted. Spiro liked dramatic moments.

"What do you know?" they all asked.

"It is the long break in Athens. When the boat comes next, Celena and Nestor return from university. They will be here with their father for six weeks."

The little group shook with merriment.

It was agreed that their pact must remain a secret. One word to somebody visiting the doctor and it would all slip out. The doctor was a man who drew his diagnoses as much from interrogation as he did from consultation. He and his wife would forbid their children from taking part in such underhand activities. That small danger aside they would be willing participants. They were smart and carefree. Everybody liked Celena and Nestor.

In his room, with a view of the little harbour, the paved walkway, the wall with stacks of nets and cane baskets and the wandering, ever vigilant seabirds, Rufus sat quietly watching. His eyes were moist. In these quiet moments, he remembered what he had done. Silently processed the events that led to his actions. Thought of the consequences. Considered all that he had forsaken in a rash moment of bravado. Nobody knew. He dared not enquire. Was he gone in the minds of those he left behind? Did they assume the worst and were now rebuilding their lives or was there a longing, a hope that it could all be made right if he were found and explanations offered?

On his lap, held loosely in his hands, the leather writer's compendium. He often held it to his face and drank in the smell of the leather. It had been a gift. Something he cherished. For its practicality, its hint of old-world mystery with the leather ties rather than a modern zip but most of all for the connection to the giver. It was now when he was alone he could not conquer the guilt.

Great art requires sacrifice he had read somewhere. The advice or perhaps confession of one who had gone before, down this same path. Had the man meant personal sacrifice or the sacrifice of decency and forsaking others in a cruel pursuit of your goals?

Now as he thumbed through the pages of his writings and little sketches he found pieces done before and then after his arrival on the island. They seemed like messages from two different worlds.

The current pad was nearly full. He had bought three for the trip. The unused other pads were left behind on the boat. His paper was a type of acid free cartridge that lent itself beautifully to a 6B pencil lead.

After a week as the cafe's waiter, Spiro called him aside one night after closing and shoved some money in his shirt pocket.

"Is not much. Sorry. I know I say bed and board only. A man must have a little money in his pocket. You seem to need clothes. It feels right. When we have good night I give you bit more eh."

Rufus took the notes from his pocket and counted them again. He would go to the shop run by the old lady with the mole on her cheek. She would smile and try to understand what the stranger was seeking. Her shop was an impressive catacomb of ancient retailing. Some items buried in its bowels were no doubt original stock from its opening day fifty years ago. Clothes that had gone right out of fashion and come back in. He may find some very suitable paper. If he failed then a Greek school exercise book would suffice.

Tonight Spiro was pressing sales of calamari. Excitement at

a particularly low price meant Rufus was instructed to buy a considerable quantity at the wharf. Not all would fit in the kitchen fridge so the remainder needed to be offloaded onto the patrons. They could have the dish pan-fried with lemon or dusted with flour, pepper and salt then fried with pieces of bread, grilled with olives and goat cheese or even stuffed and served with a creamy black ink sauce. Spiro was open to any reasonable menu suggestion as long as it involved calamari.

He held off watering the white wines in the hope that judgement would be impaired and some would order a second dish.

"Why do you only water down the whites?"

Spiro looked at his waiter. "Only the ladies drink the white. Men drink the red. Against my principles to interfere with red wine."

His first impression was that they were French tourists. She did not look like a local Greek and he was too slim and worldly. There was an elegance that suggested more sophisticated origins. They were accompanied by Kristo Eliopoulos the skipper of the Galatea, the little freighter that did the weekly run around the nearby islands, taking and bringing freight, parcels, food and supplies. He was large and overweight and enjoyed food, wine and gossip. With his inter-island connections, he was the font of most stories and innuendo that drifted through the neighbourhood.

Spiro emerged from his kitchen and grabbed Rufus by the arm.

"Ah, my good friend Kristo has arrived. Quick, sell him a double-sized calamari. And the young people too," he added as an afterthought.

"Who is the girl ...... ?"

"Go."

Spiro nudged Rufus gently toward the couple as if there were competition for their order and he must be first to arrive.

Rufus did his best to mumble a dreadfully worded Greek sales pitch for the calamari while the sea captain and his guests looked on with a valiant attempt to disguise their amusement. At its conclusion he waited then the girl spoke. With an elegant finger she brushed her long brown hair away from her beautiful face and fixing Rufus with two deep brown, sympathetic eyes she said, in exquisite English ....

"Would it be easier for you if we ordered in English?"

"They'll all have your calamari with the bread. Kristo also wants a large salad with many cheeses, oil and chillis. Oh and a bottle of Xinomavro but not that Peloponnesian rubbish."

Spiro looked askance at Rufus as he scribbled down the order on his list.

"Damned cheek of that Kristo. Once a man travels he learns too much. Give him the Assyrtiko, that should shut him up."

Rufus hovered. He looked through the kitchen door to the diners.

"Odd that a man of rather limited appeal should be dining with a young couple such as that," he opined.

Spiro smiled as he bent over his two large skillets of bubbling calamari. In a rehearsed casual manner he said, "Oh that's Celena, the daughter of doctor Anastas and his son Nestor. They are home for the University break. They would have borrowed a ride on Kristo's boat. No doubt they're buying him dinner as a thank you. They are real nice like that I am told. I believe she speaks a little English maybe, so does the boy. You should talk with them. You know, practice you English talking for them."

Rufus looked again across the tables to where the exquisite young girl smiled and chatted in a most friendly manner to the people around her. The boy was in an animated conversation with the wife of the town's motor mechanic. A man who spent most of his time fixing boat engines due to the limited number of automobiles on the island.

"Yes, maybe I will," Rufus said.

Spiro smiled again. His eyes narrowed. The free meal for Kristo and those kids would pay dividends.

It was over a week before the conspirators could assemble to hear what the girl Celena had to say.

They met on Kristo's boat late at night, each man slipping aboard via the shadows, avoiding the big lights on the wharf area.

Celena looked sparkling in the dim cabin of the captain. The men admired her beauty and her youth. All the more striking set against the dark polished timber and brass of the old ship's interior. The boy Nestor let his sister take charge. She was nineteen while he was only eighteen.

"He is a nice man," she began, "why do you want to know his secrets?" She stopped and those listening realised she wanted answers.

"A man appears in our town and asks for a room. We quickly find out that he did not come on any of our boats. There is no other way. How did he arrive? And why? It is for our security to know these things."

Spiro sat back looking pleased with his answer.

Celena laughed.

"What security? We have fish, olives, lemons, some sheep and goats. And one very bored policeman who weekly puts on weight at your cafe Spiro. Nothing happens here."

The men all answered as if in a choir.

"That is why we want to know. Nothing happens here. This is something."

"Very well," said Celena, folding her arms, "I'll tell you what my little my brother and I know but we feel bad about our duplicitous roles."

The men frowned at the meaning of duplicitous but stayed silent for fear of interrupting the girl when she was about to impart some real information.

"His name is Rufus. I have not had success in finding more than that. His notebooks are because he writes. His writing is very good. Very thoughtful. He also sketches. His drawings are also very good. He is gathering notes. Little word sketches of people, places and things that happen. I must assume that he will use his notes for a book or books. Many authors do this. It gives them a base to invent characters. Or he could be going to write non-fiction. Such as travel to little known places.

We have walked with Rufus around town and around our hills. He is a gentleman. He will talk wisely of many things but never of himself or his past. He asks lots of questions. It is hard for us to ask things when we're always answering. When we do manage a question that may lead to information about his history he becomes quiet. I think he is very sad. Perhaps a tragedy has befallen him or he has done something wrong and is suffering guilt."

Celena had stopped.

"Is that all you have?" the men asked.

Celena frowned.

"We invited him to lunch with my parents. My father likes him. Says he feels he is on a pilgrimage, a mission. Rufus had bought a school exercise book from the shop. He said it was all they had. My father was able to give him a large supply of thick cream paper left in an old desk he bought from Athens. He was very grateful."

Nestor suddenly spoke. Everybody in the cabin turned to

look at him. Some had forgotten he was there.

"The key is his notebooks. I've read his notes. They are beautiful. Such delightful insights into people and places. Parts of existence that others would miss. They are written by a man who notices things and delights in what he sees. But ..... "

Everybody waited while Nestor enjoyed his moment.

Of holding the room to ransom.

"They don't start on our island," he finally said. "They start on Santorini and then there are notes from Anafi. I'm sure there are other notebooks that came before, perhaps many. Before the one he carries with him. Rufus is a traveller who has somehow become stranded on our island. Why? That's the question I would be asking."

It was a quieter night at Spiro's. By 9.30pm even the fishermen who had come back to the harbour late were finishing their meals.

It amused Rufus as he sat in the corner with his notebook, full of fresh cream paper, that most of the fishermen ate fish for dinner. Perhaps, he mused, it was a sense of loyalty to their trade. Their way of showing support. Or perchance it had never occurred to them to eat anything else.

Rufus sketched the rugged head of Ezio as he placed large amounts of food into his mouth, chewed, talked and used his fork as a pointer to make his arguments on whatever subject the men had chosen for the night's discussion and dissection.

His own evening meal had been an extravagance. Spiro coyly admitted that Rufus had paid off his debt two weeks ago. He gave his waiter some cash and said he would receive a small wage on top of his rent and food from now. Also he could choose anything on the menu, instead of the cheap stuff. Rufus had lamb chops and fried eggs. Spiro even gave him a drinkable wine.

The breakthrough came unexpectedly.

It had been a particularly hot day. The blue waters in the bay shimmered in the bright cloudless day. Island activity moved slower than usual.

Early in the evening, before the crowds had left the harbour to make their way up the short street to Spiro's establishment, Tassos the island's entire police force, arrived at the cafe.

"What the hell you doing here?" said Spiro, looking out from the kitchen. "You left your post early? There could be a crime wave."

Both men laughed heartily.

"Where the Rufus person?"

"He's upstairs I think. Is okay, his Greek is still terrible. You can talk freely." Spiro's eyes narrowed. "Do you know something? He a criminal mastermind? What?"

Tassos reached to the top pocket of his uniform.

A place where he kept his notebook for jotting down misdemeanours. He opened the notebook and withdrew a folded sheet of paper. Unfolding it he showed it to Spiro. "What you think eh?"

"Oohh. This is very strange," Spiro replied, his finger over his lips.

It was a busy night. It seemed that all the regulars and the not so regulars decided it was time to eat at Spiros. Normally this would make Spiro very happy but tonight he was agitated, as if he had other things on his mind. Each time Rufus arrived in the kitchen with new orders the man would look at him darkly as he relayed the customer's wishes. When the rush subsided and the evening grew late with only the old men playing cards or checkers left in the yard, Spiro announced that he was going to see a fisherman about obtaining a special fish.

This was odd, as Rufus now did all the running about ordering, fetching and conveying to do with the harbour and their supplies.

"Is very special fish," said Spiro. You wouldn't understand." He left in a hurry.

At short notice not all the conspirators could assemble at the dock. Under one of the big floodlights they huddled together, fanning themselves against the hot night air and discussing the many possibilities for their need to assemble.

Tassos raised his hand and they all fell silent. Still dressed in his police uniform they watched multiple lines of sweat trace their way down his cheeks from under his hat.

"Is easy you just read this," he mumbled, handing out the piece of paper from his notebook.

Many gasps came from the crowd as they, in turn, scrutinised the contents of the official police bulletin.

It was Kristo who summed up the problem.

"We are not looking for a body. This Rufus is alive and working as we speak at Spiros. Why would they think he is dead?"

Tassos grabbed the paper and pointed to its wording.

"Because he was lost overboard from a passing yacht. It says that thing right here. He drowned."

"He looks awfully in good health for a drowned dead man. How you explain that, Mr Tassos, policeman?"

"Well, I can't. There are many possibilities. An arch-criminal, faking his own death, an international spy wishing to hide out, a man of mystery. Maybe some woman out for his genitals. I will make some initial enquiries. I have a friend in Athens, in the filing section. He will know a thing or two."

So the group disbanded. It was a decision not to tell Celena or Nestor for the sake of their safety, if some of their questioning led to Rufus reverting to character and slaying them on the spot.

"Did you arrange for that special fish?"

Spiro looked confused.

"The one you went out to organise last night."

"Oh, Ah," said Spiro, patting Rufus on the shoulder.

"Yes, it is all fixed and plans are underway."

"What sort of a fish is it? Who's it for?"

Spiro looked a little exasperated.

"Is called Galumbino. Surprise for doctor."

"Is it his birthday? Never heard of the fish. I'll look it up."

Spiro bowed his head noticeably.

"No, we just want to do something nice for the doctor. Won't be listed in your dictionary. Local name. When you going to the markets?"

Spiro watched Rufus depart.

"He is spy," he muttered. "Asks too many questions."

After two days Tassos met the group again under the floodlight. Spiro used his 'special fish' excuse again with less conviction.

"Nobody at the harbour has heard of the Galumbino," Rufus revealed.

When Spiro went an odd colour and said, "They're fools, they know nothing," Rufus backed off the subject.

Celena and Nestor were at the meeting. The secret had lasted less than an hour from their last meeting.

Tassos raised his hand the crowd fell silent, more from curiosity than respect for the law.

"My friend in Athens rang me this afternoon. He wanted to

know why I was interested in this person. I told him I needed some gossip for the local cafe. To give us something to talk about. He was okay with that."

He paused, savouring the moment. Never had he felt so in control of a crowd.

"Rufus is not a spy or a bad guy, he's a designer in the textile industry. His name is Rufus Fulverton. He and his wife and their children were having a holiday on a yacht, sailing through our Greek Isles. According to his wife he wants to be a travel writer. They had a huge argument about that very thing while sailing past our island. She went to bed. Next morning he was not on board. She has assumed that after such a long time and hearing nothing, that he is dead. Fell overboard and drowned. So they hope we might find a body."

Tassos was about to resume when Kristo spoke.

"That is very disappointing. I wanted a gangster at least. The only interesting thing now is why and how did he arrive here? Also why he say nothing or try to contact his lovely wife and beautiful children."

Somebody in the crowd made a point.

"How do we know about the lovely and beautiful? She could be ugly and a scold and the children terrible."

Celena stepped forward. She had a way of gaining attention.

"This has gone too far. Tomorrow night we trap him in the cafe yard and we make him confess. I'll bring my father to ensure it is handled in a dignified manner with a minimum chance of psychological damage."

There seemed to be a very large crowd at the cafe.

Rufus found Spiro in the kitchen.

"Nobody is ordering anything. They're all saying they'll eat later."

A brief cold shiver ran up Spiro's back. He had not considered the consequences. At 7pm the Rufus intervention was to take place. The man would no doubt be a human wreck after he was exposed. Who would wait on the tables? This evening could be financially unkind.

Perhaps Celena would help him out this evening? After all the whole thing was her idea. He looked at Rufus through narrowed eyes and shrugged.

When Dr Anastas entered the cafe with his son and daughter, Rufus felt a little uneasy. There was something odd about the atmosphere. The doctor rarely came to the cafe and there was certainly no 'special' fish in the kitchen.

The doctor walked straight up to Rufus, the crowd parting as he progressed. He said, "My dear fellow, I have come to see you. To see how you're getting on. I would like to have a chat."

Rufus was further uneased.

"I have to look after the orders and the tables."

The doctor and Celena and Nestor guided the waiter to a seat.

"Don't worry, that is all taken care of, my friend."

Now Rufus was seriously concerned. He seemed to be the centre of everybody's attention.

As all those present in the cafe courtyard gathered round, Rufus suspected his life was going to have alterations thrust upon it.

He cried. It was to be expected. For Greeks a man who cries is strong and virtuous. They could all see that he was a good man. Despite his terrible crime, their hearts went out to him. When the doctor had shown him and the surrounding people a large photo of the wife and children of Rufus, the man crumbled and became a poor, sad shaking figure.

As some admired the family portrait they were heard to say that the wife of Rufus was indeed lovely and the children beautiful. How could he do such a thing?

"I was going to go back to them," he cried. "I love them. It's …. it's that I decided that night to prove that I could be the person I wanted to be. If I could take a break and gather enough material I would be able to find a publisher and fulfil my aspirations. It would all be settled. They would understand and be happy."

"In the meantime Rufus you have a grief-stricken family who think you are dead?" Dr Anastas shook his head as he spoke. This intervention was taking place in the English language, thus a great deal of explaining and interpreting was taking place. Celena and Nestor would translate the conversation which then required further discussion and commentary in Greek. It became quite animated.

"No, no," said Rufus, "I left a note on the deck."

Dr Anastas raised his hands biblically in exasperation.

"Where did you leave this alleged note, Rufus?"

Rufus looked up at his tormentor.

"Alleged? I tucked it into the ropes holding one of the life preservers. It would have been obvious to anybody walking along the deck."

"Ah, a note," said the crowd, following translation. "Well at least he let everybody know."

"You left a flimsy note on a windy deck at night, stole one of the yacht's dinghies and rowed away to our island. Rufus, what were you thinking?"

Dr Anastas clapped his hands together as if summarising the whole sorry mess.

Rufus was silent. The crowd grew quiet. Would he cry again? Then he spoke, slowly, seriously and with great passion.

"You're right of course doctor and I thank you for your assistance in bringing this matter to my attention. It had not occurred to me that the note may have never been received. I assumed my wife would be angry but accept that I was doing what I wanted and my actions would settle this matter. I considered that she would probably be glad that my plan was finally put to the test. I am devastated by the news that they think me dead. I can only hope that in time they will forgive me and we will be a united family once more."

Rufus looked up and slowly round at all the faces gathered to watch, then he added.

"I did not steal a dingy. I swam to your shore with my notebook and sandals in a plastic bag for buoyancy." Strangely, it was not the heartfelt confession of the waiter Rufus that took the interest of the crowd, it was his epic swim from the channel to the harbour of their town. All those present were highly impressed and the status of Rufus was restored greatly.

Spiro has a new waiter these days. He is a local youth who did not want to be a fisherman and has no plans to make his future in Athens. He is not as much fun as Rufus nor as mysterious but he speaks Greek and that is a blessing.

If by chance you stop on the little island and decide to venture a meal at Spiro's Cafe you will eat well, be surprised at the moderate price, be a subject of conversation and curiosity because they still do not get many visitors and be curious yourself that the cafe has books for sale. Only two. 'Spiro's World - inside the soul of a Greek Island" and the equally successful and famous travel book, 'My Family and The World.'

Buy them and leave. Do not get talking to the cafe owner about the author. It will be a long night.

THE DAY AFTER

His uncle, it is said, while in the Emergency bed, pulled his wife close to his mouth and whispered hoarsely, "Have them finish me now."

Was this a cry of misery, of all hope abandoned or was it the realisation that his many years of flippancy and dismissal of his various doctor's urgent pleas regarding his lifestyle and its relation to his well-being?

Whatever the motive for his last-minute request it was of little consequence. Nature does not like to be neglected by some being who thinks that the laws of life and existence do not apply to them or their body's continued functioning. Following his last pointless utterances, Uncle Ralph slid quietly into a state of silence and thereafter, only some fifteen minutes later, nature did indeed carry out his final request.

At which point Aunt C stood, patted her late husband's cheek, gave a half-smile to the attending doctor and said, quite firmly, "Well, that's that over with."
She then moved to the corridor and the hospital car park while searching for her keys in her always voluminous shoulder bag.
This may have appeared to those who were present at the great man's final moments, a rather callous act, implying a lack of compassion on the part of his wife of over 50 years. However, those who knew the couple and their relationship knew that they were just a pragmatic pair who accepted life and the inevitability of death as part of the whole deal.
"Once born," he said, sometime before, to his nephew, "we are already on the road to death. It is the length of the road that has some gravitas."
He paused at the time, looked sideways, as he often did when taken by some muse and added, "That's rather good, y'know. I may use that. A baby is born with a death sentence. Oh yes."
He scribbled the words in a little brown notebook he carried at all times.

Ralph Malecent was revered. He was an old-school poet.

His work rhymed mostly. It sounded eloquent when read aloud by persons of good delivery and rich tones. His phrases had beauty. Many a word, line or piece could be remembered by school children and adults, as their little piece of culture, captured while in an early stage of learning.

Now he was gone.

Newscasts would carry the sad tidings, newspapers would run pages of obituaries, parliamentarians would rehearse and then deliver moving tributes and quote their favorite Malecent moments.

To Noel Malecent, unknown nephew and bemused observer of his uncle over the past twenty years, the dead man in the bed beside him was a massive ego gone to rest. At last.

Even in death, he filled the room. The hospital staff seemed afraid to enter as if there was insufficient space.

They had all retreated. Perhaps they had decided that as the only other relative of Ralph Malecent present at his death, he should be captured and held for a dignified period, in case he too would just off in the same manner as the wife.

They drew the curtains around the nephew and the bed and closed the door to the room. He was trapped.

As he sat looking at the sunken cheeks, manic hair and unkempt beard at the end of Ralph's jutting chin he recalled the perhaps most embarrassing moment he had spent with this uncle.

They were in a department store proceeding up some escalators. Shoppers passing on the downward escalator recognised Ralph's craggy profile and made noises of adulation. This was too much for the man and his enlarged self-esteem.

At the top of their escalator, Ralph stopped, leaving just enough room for following passengers to squeeze past. He then placed a hand on his nephew's shoulder turning him into a living lectern and with his other hand and his eyes pointing skyward he began, with that booming, unique voice to deliver one of his most famous creations.

Noel had briefly discovered prayer. It had no effect. He was not delivered from the man's grasp or the situation until thankfully the only medium length epic was completed and he received a reasonably enthusiastic pattering of applause from various floors.

"Let's be gone," he then squeezed from the side of his mouth. "They'll want autographs and ask bothersome questions."

They hid together, mostly in silence, in a men's change room for fifteen minutes.

The great man said, "I'd like a whisky and beer when we're out of here. Or is it a beer and a whisky? It will be my shout."

While drinking their whisky and beer he added, "Fame is a curse Noel, try to avoid it."

Noel agreed to do his best.

When he did leave the hospital that evening a small group of the more desperate reporters were still waiting in ambush. No doubt he had been grassed by a hospital employee.

"Noel," they called. "Noel Malecent. A few words?"

He stopped. What harm could it do? He was polite, not one to treat people with disdain as his famous uncle was wont to do.

The questions flowed. The usual mix aimed at finding a few lines that could be strung together into a press article.

Now a TV crew had a camera trained on him and their lights flick on. They reflected off the hospital's glass doors.

He was moved to the side to a non-reflective area and the little press gaggle surrounded him.

"What was it like being close to the great man?"

"Was he as warm and caring as he appeared?"

What?

"Are there any fond memories he would like to share?"

"How will the country continue without his amazing talent?"

He answered in a non-committal way, cleverly avoiding any hint of controversy or a line that could lead to a difficult follow-up question.

Then, in a flat moment when the interview seemed to be running out of steam.

What did Noel do? Was he following in his illustrious uncle's footsteps or did he have an ordinary job?

A little silence ensued. It was, after all, a rather tactless question. The enquirer looked suitably abashed.

Noel Malecent paused. He smiled enigmatically. It was a point which in the machinations of human existence could have drifted either way.

Twenty years of being the hand-maiden to the great man. Chosen by some vile lottery to be the favoured nephew and thus never left alone. Escorting him around the country at his wish and whim. Getting him safely to his room when a lone and drunk Ralph Malecent would have caused a scene and been struck down by public opinion. Being seen with him constantly but never noticed.

He could choose to dismiss the question, thank the media for their time and politely exit to his car, his home, his wife,children and a rather nice, peaceful life.

However, time was made for this moment.

"Of course I do have work of my own. Quite a large volume of work in fact. I am a Malecent after all."

He could barely believe he had uttered these words only hours after the end of RM. But now he had spoken. They could not be withdrawn. Somewhere in some distant editing suite a bored tech was looking at the TV camera signal and thinking he might have something of a splash for the late news.

That same reporter was reinvigorated.

"When would we see some of this new generation Malecent material? Could he give us a sample of a Noel Malecent piece?"

Once again, a crossroads. Walk away and let the situation resolve itself. Perhaps, in time, there might be an opening for some of the many 'pieces' he had penned over many years. Often while waiting about for his uncle. An uncle who had remained oblivious to his nephew's outpourings.

Yes, he could. He had some pages with him. Would they like to hear some?
Of course they would. (If it was rubbish then they'd simply drop the whole story.)
The cameraman lined him up, adjusted his focus and framing and gave a little finger gesture to indicate he was ready.
Noel Malecent was gifted with a particularly pleasant mid-range male voice. It had an underlying rumble but also a delightful softness that made it a pleasure to hear.
The poem was not overly long. It combined, hope, longing, love and cheer tinged with a hint of melancholy.

In Ralph Malecent's day, the road to success was arduous. It took years of dedication and constant attention to the audience to achieve notoriety.
Noel Malecent lived in the age slick media, fast and hungry media. A media that needed to be fed.
The next day on breakfast television across the country on a slow news day, Noel Malecent's poem was repeated endless-ly.
By midday, it was being recited by people to their friend's

and versions were being

posted on social media. The word they use in the trade is
'viral.' It's mostly luck. Timing is what makes or breaks these
moments. The world is shallow so it takes very little to fill
the void. Commentators used the word 'zeitgeist' to describe
the work.

Two weeks later Noel Malecent had many deals involving,
books, tours, speaking engagements, live TV appearances
and overseas functions. Famous people and politicians wanted to be seen with him. He was the star at his uncle's funeral.

Before he headed away on his first foreign engagements as
the author of 'that poem' he made a point of visiting Aunt C.
She greeted him warmly. They sat together on her terrace.
It had many pot plants and overlooked a small green valley.
With a fine bottle of Chablis and some crackers and cheese,
he waited till the small talk had subsided, then asked the
question.

"Are you upset by all this Aunt C? It was not my intention to
jump into the limelight. I'm frankly amazed by it all.
I'll understand if you're unhappy."

Aunt C continued looking at her little valley, wine glass in
hand. He waited, unable to read her expression. The lady
began to gurgle. She had only recently dispensed with her
smoking habit. Her voice contained a certain rasping edge.
She was laughing. Her laughter grew to quite a pitch. It took
minutes and a couple more shots of Chablis for her to attain

calmness. She looked at Noel.

"Ah my dear boy, I couldn't be happier." She stopped for another sip of wine.

"Ralph would be so annoyed. That's what makes the situation so adorable. I loved dear Ralph from the day we met to the day he died. I still do. We enjoyed each other and although we had no children, life did give us many pleasures. He said to me once that he'd had a sneak look at some of your jottings.

Talented little bastard, he said, but he'll never make a go of it. Doesn't believe. You need belief.

My Ralph had a massive ego. He believed that much hard work was the only way to succeed. He didn't think you were capable of hard work. And as I know you're thinking it, I'll say, that being with Ralph itself was hard work. He didn't notice that.

If you want my opinion you'll do well. But it will be brief. Make lots of money while you can. Our current world wants a new hero every day. Nobody wants yesterday's hero. Ralph lasted a lifetime. I'll give you a year."

THE ARRANGEMENT

The boy liked to hold my hand. He gave me that sad, I don't understand look when I told him he could not do so unless we were a long way from the town.

Could he be my son? of course. It is possible, though a close observer might find it odd, despite his tender appearance belying his years.

I tried to discourage excursions, even when we travelled considerable distances to seek some freedom, there was still a chance that we may have been seen by a person who pondered our circumstance.

For quite some time after he became my responsibility, we managed a degree of comfort and normality in our relationship. When that changed he enjoyed the situation and tried his best to be mature and bring a level of understanding as to how it could all be lost if he were careless.

I wonder if I thought it could find a way to simply run its course. An episode that would move on once time proved it no longer useful or fulfilling. Like a drunkard driving on a country road, I saw no obstacles of note and enjoyed the scenery, unaware of the inevitability of my continuation of the journey.

He was a scholarship boy. The college gave out two per year. A nice but largely unwelcome necessity for the board of governors to be seen as altruistic and reaching out to the broader community. In large, they treated the SB's well. However, there was an underlying pecking order in many aspects of a scholarship boy's progress and their access to certain of the college's privileges.

I had been at the school for a year. It was one of four where I assisted as a counsellor. In my case, a degree in psychology and other background training aided my acceptance and salary. This particular appointment carried some prestige. The college had a 'name.'

I was the sole person in charge of all the college boys welfare. Not an onerous task. In general, the pupils were comfortable, happy, well-adjusted products of wealthy families. They all had relaxed, comfortable futures on their horizons.

I moved to the town and devoted much time into
establishing myself within their system. After six months,
feeling secure I resigned from two of my other four posts.

That same year, was what the Governor called a 'bumper
crop'. Enrolments were up quite dramatically. While there
was an established system for booking a place, almost from
a child's birth, money and importance could and was used to
jump the line.

At a meeting with the board which I was asked to attend,
the members wrestled with the problem of a full list of
dormitories. They were close to having their dilemma
defeated. Except for one.

"There's the two SBs," they said. "Obviously full paying
pupils must take precedence over these fellows who are here
at the largess of the college. But what to do?

Now several of our senior boys have secured digs in the
town. They like the freedom and their parents are happy
to pay but we still don't have any dorm room for the
Scholarship Boys. A local family says they will take one of
the lads and we have no idea what to do with the other."

"Which boy will the family take?" I asked.

They looked at me.

"Well, that is where you come in. In your role here, you
have spoken to both boys. Can you give us any guidance as
to what can be done? Tell us. Which boy would best suit a

family environment and then perhaps a suggestion or two as to what we might do with the other?"

I now knew why I had been asked to attend their meeting. I was not being asked for academic advice, I was being used to give them a course of action that would clear them of any possible ramifications if the board's decision were ever questioned.

One SB was from a family with names and titles. They had fallen on hard times and were quite poor. The other boy was a sweet, academically gifted product of a family where the mother had died and the father was always overseas.

I did what they wanted. I recommended the titled boy for the family situation. It was a pact that no doubt had already been made between the college and the family seeking a little glamour.

As for the other boy, I was at a loss.

The board members sat stroking their chins, looking about. One drummed his fingers. Another cleared his throat unnecessarily. What was I missing?

Finally one of them took up the challenge.

"You see there's just nobody to take him on. It would be a dreadful shame if we were forced to cancel his scholarship over such a trivial matter. We have put in a considerable amount of effort searching for a placement. He's far too young to be in digs by himself. None of the senior lads have room. We could supplement a placement but we could not justify paying full board for the lad, even if a suitable place were found."

Perhaps I was naive but still, I was missing their point.

A point that in retrospect was so obvious.

The men did their thought and puzzlement charade once more. Then, seeing I was not rising to their bait, they spoke.

"You know, something has just occurred to me. It is unusual but it might just work. Needless to say, it is a last resort and I only bring this up because of the dire situation."

He paused. Of course. Suddenly I knew where the whole process was headed. Finally, the man blurted it out.

"My dear, would you consider taking the lad on? As you know we are aware of your live-in partner's departure and I believe from what you've told us there is no chance of reconciliation. He has left your life completely, you say. Now you live in a large house. Perhaps having this delightful young chap under your care might provide some outlet for your spare time and provide a little companionship."

He paused, before plunging on with his pitch.

"What do you say? It would help us and the lad out immensely and as I said we'd be happy to provide a generous supplement to ensure you were fully compensated."

Two months after the boy's arrival we were sitting on the wide front verandah deck. It was Spring and the first hint of warm weather had arrived that morning. By default it was a place we now sat together on weekends.

It was the same place where my now departed partner and I had spent so much idle time. I had been so content. We had such a wonderful, carefree relationship. In retrospect another example of some naivety on my part. I had considered the man to be happy, totally missing the signals. Until the day he announced he would be returning to the city, that the quiet life in the country was not to his taste. He was sorry and concerned for me but not enough to delay his departure. We remained friends and he rang me occasionally to talk and make pleasant promises of a visit that never seemed to fit with his schedule. I missed his companionship and the included intimacy very much.

The boy was a dream. He was bright of nature, intelligent without the accompanying sense of entitlement that often comes with brainpower. Clean, neat and tidy and great company. In a conversation, I often forgot that he was thirteen and I was thirty-one. No awkwardness, no stumbling, looking for words. We explored lofty ideas and simple facts with equal enthusiasm. Perhaps he had not previously had a person with whom to make conversation or if he had, they were always adults. So the transition was never a challenge.
Most of all the boy was appreciative. He understood this lifeline he held and he seemed to want it to succeed. Occasionally, after a nice meal or when I helped him out in some way, he would stop and hug me tightly for a second

and whisper, "Thank you."

He rarely made contact with his father and when they did talk the man always seemed to be on the way to or from someplace far away. I spoke to him once and he thanked me for looking after the boy. It sounded like a man who had found a good boarding kennel for his pet Labrador.

The boy's schoolwork progressed nicely and I continued my work in counselling some of the vaguely troubled pupils in the other locale I serviced. Mostly with very simple cases of anxiety, a little peer pressure or a bad grade.

Today, with the warm weather, the boy wore only some shorts and a t-shirt. He sat in one of our two large wooden deck chairs, intermittently sipping a cold drink, absorbed in a book.

I looked at him. Legs stretched out, bare feet. There was a natural warm glow about him. He had faintly brown skin. His limbs were perfect. His slender fingers held the book with such reverence. A tiny frown flickered on his face as he scanned the text.

I was absorbed in my inspection when he looked up and gave me a most disarming and genuine smile.

My heart jumped. From being caught out or by the realisation of what a beautiful child I observed? From the thick brown curls of hair laying on his neck to the deep pool of his eyes, he was quite angelic.

He would be fourteen late this year but he looked younger. A lost child.

It was just a moment and life continued however I did quietly
analyse my feelings toward my charge. I decided I was
showing signs of motherly instincts and that my admiration
and indeed affection for the boy were natural manifestations
of our being in close proximity to each other. While I made
a point of giving him personal space and keeping my
suggestions or commentary to a minimum I noted he did not
necessarily give me the same in return. He thought nothing
of wandering in to ask me a question while I was half-dressed
or reviewing my driving technique at times when I dropped
him to the school.

There were several instances while I was showering, he had
knocked at the door urgently needing to pee. With a towel
wrapped round me I would let him in and stand while he
sighed and let it all rush out.

Once he asked to invite a school-friend over for the day.
The boy was a pleasant sandy-haired character whose father
was a merchant banker. His disposition was that of a person
with not a care in the world and therefore no need to have
any graces, habits, inhibitions or for that matter opinions on
anything. It was this outgoing easy nature that had attracted
my boy but as they spent a whole day together it became
obvious that this was also the reason why they had so little
in common. Nothing fulfilling was taking place.

To save the situation I took them for a drive to a river. We
hired a boat and the boys took turns in rowing along the

river shore.

When next I asked my boy if he'd like to have another friend over he replied, "Not really. I just like being with you."

When was the moment? There is an answer of course. It had to do with his dreams.

His room was two doors away on the other side of the hall. His window faced the yard.

At night he would be absorbed in a book. I would see his light on and knock.

"Hoy you, sleep time. School tomorrow."

He'd answer, "Yes, boss," and his light would go out.

Lately, I noted the 'Yes boss," had changed to "Yes," and my name. I let it go. After a while, he called me by my first name all the time. I rather liked it. Part of our informal relationship. Other nights his light would be out and sometimes I heard whimpering. At first, alarmed, I opened his door and listened. It became apparent that he just had vivid dreams and seemed to vocalise the events in his head.

I mentioned it in the morning and he simply said, "Did I? Wow. Don't know what it was. Can't remember anything."

Summer came. The house was hot. We left doors open to allow some air movement.

I heard a loud cry, then another.

He wasn't in his bed. When I flicked on the light he was standing in the hall, his back against the wall. He was shaking. He looked at me as if he was unsure of his location. When I walked up I lifted his face. He was confused. I hugged him to me and stroked his hair.

"You must have had one of those monster dreams my friend."

"Yes," he muttered. Then, "Monster or something."

I rubbed his back. He wore only sleepshorts. He was wet with sweat.

Sitting beside him on his bed while he sipped a glass of water I continued to rub his back.

"If I didn't know what a level-headed, smart guy you were I'd be worried about you. Life can't be that hard. I think you just have a very strong imagination."

We sat for some minutes. When he had calmed I suggested he'd be alright.

"Can you rub my back some more? That's really nice."

Later in my own bed I considered the situation.

"No mother, father always away. He must crave human contact. Just being touched would be very comforting for a being so deprived of such experience. I made a note to give him the occasional hug, even a kiss on the cheek. He would like that.

It happened four nights later. A Saturday evening. Quite warm with a slight warm breeze that did nothing to cool the air.

I lay on my bed with just a sheet on top. Sleep was fitful but I had drifted into a slumber.

There was movement and noise in the dark. Something touched me. I started and stared into the darkness, trying to make sense of what was happening. He was in my bed, shaking and clinging to me.

"It happened again," he said. "It happened again. Hold me."

This time I held him close and told him to relax. Feeling his skin, his body against mine. It was not unpleasant.

I waited. To hold him was so nice.

After a few minutes his breathing slowed and I could feel the tension run from his body. His breathing eased still more and he sighed. I turned and stroked his forehead. He seemed at peace. There was a point where I felt that calm was restored and I could guide him back to his bed and let him rest. We should talk about these dreams in the morning. It was good to have somebody for whom I could care. Perhaps some medication may help.

I lent over so that I could kiss his cheek saying,

"What am I going to do with you?"

He turned his face and our lips met.

That was the moment. I did not pull away.

Did he plan it? Was it simply an accident in timing? Did I let it happen?

Anytime after that I could have called out and stopped what happened but as the kiss was so soft, so complete and lingering, so needful, as we explored each other's bodies, his involvement did not waver. As I guided him, took him to me, as he let out little whimpers of ecstasy, as I felt his beautiful, hairless skin, his helplessness and need, I gave in to every hint of sense and clarity and made it all happen.

There was a second, less viable chance. In the morning, when I woke and found this boy beside me, I could have taken charge, rectified things, made him understand and made arrangements. However, I was neither horrified or ashamed. Instead, I looked down at his beautiful face lying still and asleep on the white pillow and I was overcome. We repeated the night all over again with more joy and reassurance.

Now, in late summer, he has started to say he loves me. I have done nothing to deter our relationship. Despite all my training, my professional position, I continue to let it run. What are my feelings? What lies beneath the surface? Do I love him in that way or just want him?
Is this wrong or is society wrong? I continue to find ways to justify our relationship. It is convenient and I cannot find in myself the strength to bring it to an end.
He's a child, very intelligent, able to understand mature concepts and the need for immense care but that does not overcome raw, immature emotion on his part.
It is out of control.
Now I am scared.

The woman whose opinion will decide my long-term situation has two sessions with me each week.

It is a battle of wits. She is torn between her professional opinion and her knowledge that, with my training, I could simply be feeding her answers she needs to hear and in fact I have made no progress at all.

I am tempted to try a frank, 'we're both professionals here' approach but I suspect that would not serve me well. There could not be a crossing of boundaries. I am the inmate and she is the arbiter of my fate.

The single overriding factor appears to be my chances of re-offending. There are so many answers I do not use.

"No, of course not. It is not in my nature. I am at a loss to process why I let it happen in the first place. Besides with all my employment terminated, the publicity, the news reports, my career ruined, no prospect of any further work in my field, I fail to see when, where or how I could ever have the chance to repeat the 'crime'.

Newspaper headlines like, 'The Pretty Teacher And The Schoolboy.' Sub-head, 'Get a Little Too Close,' did not help. Even though I wasn't a teacher. The media get so many things wrong.

The boy tried to help. At the trial, he protested that it was, in fact, he who initiated the affair and almost blackmailed me into being his unwilling participant.

The prosecution and the judge took the time-honoured view that no matter what pros and cons may be presented concerning the willingness of both participants the adult in the matter should be aware and able to stop the whole thing before it ever started. They knew they were on safe legal grounds as well as covering public opinion.

They did, however, refrain from suggesting that I, as a woman, had raped the boy. I think they thought they had granted me a nice concession. Shown some compassion considering the delicate emotions at play.

Besides, our 'relationship' was far from a brief encounter. It continued for 8 months and could possibly still be in operation had not the boy's notebook been grabbed during a lunch recess and his most heartfelt personal notations been read out to a large crowd of schoolboys by some seniors, thinking it was all a huge joke.

The sentence, all considered, was light. Three years with a non-parole period of eighteen months. I am in the sex offender's wing. The female section has only four occupants. Even so, there are some very disturbing people here.

I see myself as a minor offender. I quietly laughed when that concept came to mind.

Though I can see why my case-worker is cautious.

I have said and done all the right things as best I can. Given every indication, I am back in the right frame of mind. We'll see. Eighteen months passed by a few days ago. Generally, parole is not granted on a first attempt. Possibly to appease any persons who might consider the system too soft.

He wrote to me a few weeks back. I was doubly surprised. To hear from the boy at all and that the letter appears to have passed through the system untouched.
After his expulsion from the college, his exasperated father had managed to find him a place in a down-at-heel and low-cost boarding school. He suggests they would take anybody.
Perhaps cleverly his letter is most general in nature. It offers no hint that there could be any lingering connection between us. Just a note to let me know he is well. Nothing to alert the authorities.
At the end, he says that he has created quite a lucrative, income-producing, enterprise by which he does computer trouble-shooting in the evenings. He hopes soon to be able to move out of the school dormitory into some quite comfortable and spacious lodgings in the town.
He wishes me well at the end and signs off with a 'yours truly.' Which as we all know is a normal and accepted way of ending general correspondence.

RACAKI

$\mathbf{T}$his man in the opposite seat looked old in his eyes.
He drank slowly, rolling the whisky round in his mouth, to
extract every morsel of enjoyment before swallowing.
"It has been a considerable time since I've tasted a good
whisky," he said quietly, "excuse me if I try to make it last."
The westerner seated with the Asian smiled indulgently.
"I think I can afford another," he replied, "take your time."
"Ah, time, that is something you may not be able to buy for
me."
"Are you unwell?"
"My heart. It is broken in many pieces."
"Cardiac disease?"

"No, sadness."

It had started an hour before. The westerner, wandering idly through the backstreets of this Asian city at dusk. It was an easy, untroubled walk. The place did not see tourists. There existed no mechanism to chase and exploit strangers. The man was left alone. He enjoyed the peace of the late day. The easing back of the frantic streets as the people took their leave.

At a stall selling noodle dishes, the proprietor was closing up his awning and umbrella. Locking away his cookers and dishes.

"I can give you my last scraps. Mix in bowl for you. No charge. Going to throw away."

As the stranger ate his free meal, seated on a rock wall, the noodle man finished his packing by tying a blue tarpaulin round his stand and boxes of ingredients.

The westerner spoke.

"Can I thank you for your generosity with a glass at the bar over there?" he inquired. "What drink is your favourite?"

The third whisky was purchased.

The Asian man looked guilty. "I cannot repay you. My noodles are of low cost. I make very little."

"You are paying me with your company, otherwise I would be sitting here drinking alone. It is said that nobody should drink alone. Please enjoy the whisky and let us just be friends for the night. Now tell of your life and your fortunes. Where are you from or are you a local resident?"

The Asian man shrank in his cane chair. He looked away. The whisky glass was gently placed on the little round table between the two men. A silence ensued. His eyes were no longer in the room. He seemed to have withdrawn to some distant place.

"Have I offended you?" the westerner enquired.

His evening companion returned to the room.

"No, please, not at all." He lifted his whisky glass and took another sip. "So good," he said, "you are most kind." He paused and looked at his benefactor.

"I come from Racaki. It is my wish to return but I cannot. Please do not be burdened by my troubles."

For a time the foreigner stayed silent. He looked into his glass. He wore a puzzled expression.

"My friend, I am not Asian but I have lived in this region, for many years and travelled extensively. I feel I know every town, island and small hamlet there is to offer. I do not know of Racaki."

"It is pronounced ras-a-ki. It is an island. I lived and grew in its green embrace and swam in its pearl sea in my youth. Then I grew restless and left my island. Now I wish to return but I do not know how to get back."

The foreigner smiled.

"Is it the fare you seek? Surely you make whatever travel arrangements are required and you go. I am still intrigued.

Is your island far away? It would be nice to add to my knowledge. Tell me about Racaki. Where is it and how do I get there?"

The Asian man kept his head bowed, staring at their little table.

"I don't know," he finally said.

"Don't know what?"

"Where is my island. I don't know how to get there."

The man sipped his whisky and continued.

"A deep-sea fishing boat stopped at Racaki one day. They needed a safe anchorage while they carried out some repairs. I befriended them, brought them food and water in my canoe. They paid our village well for goods. They stayed over a week. Gave me some money and other things like a knife, a fishing pole with a clicking spool and some magazines called National Geopgraphic. I walked on the decks and explored the galley and cabins. It was fascinating. One morning as I made my delivery, they said that they had fixed their boat and were about to leave. I was sad. I enjoyed this experience so much.

One of the crew said, "Why don't you come along? We need another deck-hand. It's a great life."

I had to decide right then. Their motor was running, I was sitting in my canoe and the boat was beginning to move.

The man reached down to me. I looked back at my island, to the beach and road and the huts. Here was my chance to see the world. I took his hand and he pulled me on board."

"How old were you?"

"Fifteen. When you're that age you don't think ..... of your mother and father, your brothers and sisters or the consequences of your actions. It seemed so easy. My canoe would have floated ashore. I suppose they think I drowned."

"Did you miss them?"

"Of course I did. My heart ached. After three days I cried and asked the captain to take me back home. He said that was impossible, they were too far away. They were kind. They fed me well and I had my own bunk. The work was very hard though, we had many cuts and bruises. After two months they returned to port. We had travelled a long way. I was paid for my work and a share of the catch and had to promise to be back on board in a week as they were going to head toward the south. "Out of the gulf they said,"

The foreigner ordered some snacks, soda water and more whisky.

"Please," he said, "I still do not understand. You are around 30 years of age. At 15 you had money why did you not simply go home?"

The noodle vendor picked at a bowl of small fish pieces on their table.

"You have a good eye for age, sir. I was a teenaged boy in a big town. It was terrifying. My education was limited. I did not know the ways of the world. Even basic things were a mystery to me. The other crew members stuck with me but they wanted to get drunk and chase women. I lost them.

I bought clothes, my first shoes, a big shoulder bag, even a watch. When I finally found the fishing harbour again, the boat had gone. For fifteen years I have worked in all sorts of jobs and moved to various towns. I ask all the time. Do you know Racaki? I wish to go to Racaki? All say same thing. No place called that. You mad person. Doesn't exist. Even smart people, travel people, tell no Racaki, I must imagine it."

The man's eyes were wet. He was agitated.

At 10pm the two men parted. They shook hands in the street, damp from a little evening rain. The Asian man thanked his night's companion for his company and generosity. As he walked away in the empty street the westerner watched the other man's figure outlined by neons and bar lights. He seemed hunched. His demeanour was that of a broken being. How many people had heard his story? What was the reality of his situation? The watcher rubbed his face in annoyance. It was a problem for another day, for some others to resolve. Perhaps it would never be resolved.

"Where is the noodle seller?" He pointed across the road. The barman looked past him to the empty spot on the road outside.

"He not there today. Haven't seen him."

"Do you know where he lives?"

"No. Somewhere near. He make good food. I eat often. Hope he comes back."

It was late. The westerner sat in the bar for a while watching the street and the local people.

The next day the noodle vendor's spot remained empty. On the third day the man turned the corner past the medicine shop and looked up the street. The stall was there. The barman from across the street was standing, eating and talking.

As the man approached the barman pointed with his chopsticks.

"Here he come." He turned from the noodle seller. "I tell him you look for him. Want more of his good food."

The food stand was busy. It seemed the seller really did have a talent in how he prepared, cooked and spiced his dishes. The westerner waited his turn and asked for a pork and noodle staple he knew.

"Pad kee mao?"

"Ah, drunken noodles. Yes, yes, okay. No charge."

"No, no. No free. I pay like everyone else. After, when quiet, can we talk?"

The cook stopped briefly, poised over his wok.

"Yes, sure, we can talk."

"I'll be back, mid-afternoon."

"Sure, sure."

He plunged back to his cooking, flicking in the ingredients, sauces and spices with practiced hand. In a minute the dish was ready and dropped into a bowl. It was exceptionally good.

At 3.30pm the westerner returned. There were no customers. He sat down next to the noodle seller in the shade of the cart's big umbrella. He looked the vendor in the eye and nodded.

"I've done a lot of research. I'm a journalist. I know how to find things. Racaki does not exist."

The man held up his hand to stop any protest before it could start.

"At least not in the practical world."

He paused and shrugged still looking at the other man.

"I have a theory. It may be wrong .... I believe your people, the locals who live where you once lived, might have their own name for their home. A name that is only known to them. I've come across it before. It is sometimes comfortable to have a local secret that gives an area a sense of community. Especially so on an island, I'd imagine. To the world, it is known by another name. You may have heard this other name as you grew but you don't think it is significant. A name that could find your home. Now, my friend. What is that other name? Come to the bar tonight and we'll talk. Drinks on me. There's a story here. That is my payment. Are you interested?"

The little stall closed early. As soon as there was a break in the evening customers, the man whipped down his umbrella, folded his seats and doused water on his wok. Something that would normally be considered bad form for an Asian cook. As he wrapped his tarpaulin round the whole setup a couple complained. Whatever he said they backed away, heads bowed, hands together in front. Perhaps he said there had been a death.

He arrived breathless in the bar with bowls of food for his host, the barman and himself. Tonight they were drinking beer.

At 10.30pm the man was morose. He looked at his benefactor.

"My life was and is simple. There is nothing else to tell. I can think of no other words or names. My family talked of the crops, the weather, the neighbours. I went to the village school. We learnt how to talk and read and add and subtract. My childhood was lovely but I remember nothing more."

During lulls in bar duties the barman joined them. Now aware of his customer's predicament he had dismissed his earlier skepticism of the whole Racaki story and taken on the white man's enthusiasm for the hunt.

The street was deserted when they parted. The barman locking up. All three men headed off in different directions. The noodle vendor looking even more miserable.

"It is why I have no lady," he'd said. "They all leave. You and your stupid obsession they say."

In silence, they felt his frustration.

The men parted. The street lay quiet except for the occasional buzz of a badly functioning neon sign.

Then in the distance, from the direction of the white man came a cry. It rang out and bounced off the walls and pavements.

"The boat! The bloody boat!" he screamed.

They all rushed back to meet in the street. Wild-eyed, they looked at the white man, the journalist. This foreigner had cried out. Why?

"It's so obvious. The boat, that fishing boat. It knew where it was. The crew had maps and charts. Did they ever mention a name or say a word about where they were?"

"No. We all knew."

"Well as it turns out, no you didn't."

The barman was excited.

"We just have to go to the boat and they will tell us."

Silence ensued.

"Fifteen years. Boat go to many ports. Probably sunk or sold."

The foreigner broke through the niceties of the culture and took the little chef by the shoulders. He stared into the man's eyes.

"Let's be positive," he spelled out. "Was the captain young?"

"Yes, he was."

"Then there's a chance he still sails the boat and that port where you were left. It was probably their home port. My friend, what was the name of that port?"

The barman and the whiteman stared. The noodle man's face brightened.

"Soongkharna."

"And the name of the boat?"

"Sawatdee."

"Hullo and goodbye?"

"They think it funny. Always coming and going."

This night was the last that the barman or the vendor would see the whiteman journalist. He seemed to vanish. It was sudden. Then they heard he had been posted elsewhere. They talked occasionally of that final meeting when hopes were high and with the port only 200 kilometres away, that the man would unearth the truth. It all faded.

Now the port was beyond reach. Who could go there and wait for some boat that no longer exists?

The barman sold beer and liquor and chased women. The noodle man sold his meals. He even invested in a new umbrella but then somebody stole it so he had to resume using the original.

A lady came to know the street vendor. She had a new stall nearby that sold pots, pans and cooking utensils. She wanted to cook and the vendor showed her some of his secrets.

They became friends, she helped on his stall and gave him some nice new pans and a bigger, better wok. She moved in with him.

The barman waited for the day when it would all end. The day when his friend told the lady about Racaki. This time it did not end. The lady loved the story and believed it. She said how much she would like to go to such a place and live in peace. It was a shame they would not be able.

A year passed and the street and the daily life changed very little. The man in the shop that sold TVs and watches and other items with famous brands and dubious pedigrees, was arrested for selling drugs to some white people. It was accepted that he sold drugs but white people talk too much. It would have brought trouble.

The lunchtime rush was nearing its end. Now with expanded cooking facilities the lines of customers could be quite daunting. A man stepped up to place his order. The pots and pans lady, who was helping again, smiled and asked what he required.

He smiled back most pleasantly and said, "I would like the shrimp soup. I have always liked shrimp soup. Though I think your chef stole the recipe from my cook when he was onboard the 'Sawatdee.'"

The lady looked bewildered. Somewhere in her mind she had an unnerving feeling that this was something of an important moment. That ship name, it sounded familiar. She turned to the noodle seller.

He was motionless, his head tilted as if some far off sound had caught his attention. His wooden spatulas were poised over the wok, as the contents started to smoke and burn. Then he turned his head to look at the customer and gave out a most terrifying shriek.

The feast was in its third day. Still, people came. They brought pork and chickens and fish and endless happiness. News had spread.

On their phones and devices, they communicated the amazing story of the return of the dead man. They wanted to see this lost boy who once again sat amongst them with his mother and father and brothers and sisters. They wanted to know when he would marry his lady-friend and produce more residents for their island 'Racaki'.

The man himself, the centre of all the attention, was at once bewildered, delighted, perhaps sad. The quest was over. He had achieved his dream of finding this place.

The journalist was right. Racaki was a local name for local people. The island was part of a group of over twenty islands. On the charts it was known by another name as part of the group.

His former captain presented an offer that could not be refused. Passage to his island on the fine ship 'Sawatdee II'.

The white man had visited the harbour. Knowing he could not wait perhaps months for a ship to perhaps call in, he recruited two locals who worked at the harbour and paid them to inform him of the ship's arrival. There would be a bonus for whichever watcher could arrange for him to speak to the captain. With such rivalry set in place, the chances of a successful outcome were greatly enhanced.

Eventually, after some considerable time, the fishing boat did sail into the port and tie up for a break. Things then happened quite quickly.

The captain remembered their 'stolen' island boy fondly and was happy to help in the quest. He suffered some guilt from the original actions of taking the boy from his home.

He planned to return him but the boy was lost to them.

In time, with all options considered, the street vendor and his now wife went back to the big town. They sat down and drank in the little bar and said goodbye to their barman friend. They sold their businesses, packed many pots, woks and other utensils and returned to Racaki where they built a modest house and greatly pleased the local people with their immensely popular street cafe.

Customers often asked why the man had a bottle of the finest, expensive whisky sitting high in a glass-fronted case up behind his counter.

"It is waiting for a special guest," he would reply.

"When is this guest coming?" they would ask.

"Maybe never," was all he would tell them.

And so it was.

One day, early in a bright morning, when the birds were still calling in the trees and the sound of the sea on the sand could be heard in the hush, a white man walked into the Racaki Cafe. He was holding the hand of a small boy.

"I met this young fellow outside, playing with his sister," the man said, smiling. "He says he is your son and that he will be five years old tomorrow. I have come for my story."

The proprietor closed his eyes for a moment and took a deep breath, letting it out slowly. He bowed his head while pressing his hands together in the manner of a prayer.

Then he turned and reached up, most carefully taking down the whisky bottle from the glass case.